Frederica
and the
Viscountess

Praise for Frederica and the Viscountess

"Davies does an excellent job of emulating Austen's style and mannerisms in the story of the viscountess. The influence of *Pride and Prejudice* will be obvious to any reader who is familiar with that book. The nice thing about the book is that Davies stays true to the period in dealing with the love affair between the women." — Lynne Pierce, *Piercing Fiction*

Other books by Barbara Davies . . .

Barbara Davies

Frederica
and the
Viscountess

NuAnce
Books
Bedazzled Ink Publishing Company * Fairfield, California

978-1-960373-24-3 paperback

Library of Congress Control Number: 2010908316

1st Edition 2010
2nd Edition 2024

Cover art
by

Sapling
Studio

with apologies to C. E. Block

Nuance Books
a division of
Bedazzled Ink Publishing Company
Fairfield, California
http://bedazzledink.com/books/nuance-books/

With respectful thanks to Jane Austen and Georgette Heyer for many hours of enjoyment.

CHAPTER 1

A FAIR HEAD peered round the breakfast parlour door. "You will never guess what Edmund Lynton is telling Mama and Papa."

Frederica looked up from her needlework and smiled at her younger sister. "And why should I even attempt it, since you are clearly longing to tell me."

Amelia closed the door and came to sit next to her. "She," she said, in tones of deep significance, "is coming to stay at Thornbury Park."

Frederica bit off the thread and regarded her sampler with satisfaction. "She?"

"Edmund's sister, of course."

"Viscountess Norland?" She blinked. "But I thought she was in Greece, or was it Venice?" The Viscountess's travels on the Continent had long been a favourite topic of discussion among the younger members of the Bertram family, though her activities seemed to have been less outrageous of late. A moment's reflection made Frederica realise her error. "Ah, she returned to Paris last year, did she not?"

Amelia nodded.

"No doubt Napoleon's army made it too dangerous to remain." News from across the Channel was not good. Rumour had it that the Duke had suffered a defeat.

"She is coming to visit her brother," continued Amelia.

"Very sisterly of her," said Frederica, determined to give the Viscountess the benefit of the doubt. "And very heartening to know that even she has family feelings." She put the sampler aside.

"Hah! I daresay nowhere else is willing to accept her. As for family feelings, have you forgotten?" Amelia rose to her feet and began to pace. "She deserted her husband and son."

"No," said Frederica quietly. "I have not forgotten."

Amelia came to a stop and turned to face Frederica, her arms akimbo. "You are missing the point, as always. If Viscountess Norland is to be at Thornbury Park, what will become of our visits there?"

"Why, nothing, I daresay. We shall go on as always."

"And risk meeting her?"

"I would have thought you would be eager to meet a woman as notorious as one of Mrs. Radcliffe's characters."

Amelia looked intrigued. "I had not considered it in those terms. You are right, Frederica. Her presence at Thornbury Park should provide *some* entertainment at least. Can you imagine the upset it will cause in the village?" She sighed. "Thank heavens! Sometimes, you know—in particular when Mr. Smith is here—I could scream from boredom."

Poor Mr. Smith, thought Frederica. The son of the clergyman adored her sister, but since Herbert was neither handsome nor rich, nor wore a red coat, the sentiment was not returned. Fortunately—or should that be unfortunately?—the amiable young man was also not very bright, and had yet to realise his suit was hopeless.

"Meeting the Viscountess is not very desirable, to be sure. But since we have no idea of the length of her stay, and she will no doubt have much to keep her occupied, I see no reason why matters between Chawleigh and Thornbury Park need alter in any way."

"But—"

What Amelia had been about to say was lost forever as the breakfast parlour door opened and a maid appeared.

"Your father wishes to speak to you both."

Frederica exchanged a look with her sister, and they made their way to the drawing room.

MR. BERTRAM, HANDS clasped behind his back, was standing in front of the drawing room window, gazing out at the June sunshine and the rider in the blue coat cantering away from the house.

"There you are." He turned to regard his two daughters as they took their seats on the sofa next to their mother. "I have something to say to you concerning Thornbury Park. Though"—his gaze fell on Amelia, and a small smile curved his lips—"you have likely already heard the news."

Amelia coloured at being caught eavesdropping but said nothing.

"It seems there is to be a new arrival there. Mr. Lynton informed me that Viscountess Norland—"

A muffled exclamation stopped him mid-sentence, and he turned to regard his wife. "Yes, my dear?"

"It is very hard," said Mrs. Bertram, "very hard indeed, to have that woman staying in the neighbourhood. It lowers the tone a great deal."

"She is our neighbour's sister," he said a touch sharply. "And he has been kind enough to give us advance notice." He turned to his two daughters. "Frederica. What is your opinion on this matter? You are the one most affected by this development."

She blinked. "Am I?"

"Now, now." His eyes twinkled. "Do not play the coy miss with me. You know I am referring to your talks with Mr. Dunster."

Frederica's cheeks warmed. "Yes, Papa."

At twenty-seven, she was well on her way to spinsterhood, and all too aware of it. Several offers had been made for her hand, but she had found good reason to reject them—to her own satisfaction if not to her family's. Her parents were now pinning their fading hopes on Edmund Lynton's brother-in-law. Chaloner Dunster had recently inherited Symond Hall and its four hundred acres in Norfolk, and was staying with the Lyntons while renovations were made to the run-down property.

A moderately wealthy man, now in active pursuit of a wife, was not to be sneezed at, and Chaloner had shown an interest in Frederica. She knew that her parents were counting on her to bring him to the point of making an offer. She also knew her duty. Four children had been a significant drain on her father's resources, though things were easier now that her two brothers were married.

But the thought of such a future was, as always, lowering, so she pushed it away and returned to the matter at hand.

"May we not continue as before?" she suggested. "It would be only good manners to behave amicably towards the Lyntons and the Dunsters. Should they be made to suffer for what is, after all, in the Viscountess's past? Besides, we do not as yet know how long she will be staying."

Mr. Bertram gave her an approving nod and opened his mouth to speak.

"Really, Frederica!" Mrs. Bertram was incensed. "How can you suggest such a thing? As if you should even be in the same *house* as that odious woman!"

Frederica's father raised an eyebrow at the interruption, but said mildly enough, "I trust our daughters are sensible enough not to be irrevocably harmed by her company, Mrs. Bertram."

Frederica was not so certain—Amelia could be a hoyden at times—but she held her peace.

"I was for cutting them all at first, Papa," said her sister piously, "but Frederica changed my opinion. Besides, it would be very tedious not to be able to visit Thornbury Park. I should miss playing with the dear children so."

He gave Amelia an indulgent smile. "Indeed you would. And," he looked meaningfully at his wife, "it would be unfortunate if Mr. Dunster were to forget all about Frederica, which he may very well do if she does not visit at least once a week."

"You could invite him here," said Mrs. Bertram. "Would that not serve?"

But his face had assumed the stony expression that Frederica knew well. "Viscountess or no Viscountess, we shall continue our friendly relations with those at Thornbury Park." He turned to regard his daughters. "And you two will behave in a manner that will give me no cause to regret my decision."

"Yes, Papa," chorused Frederica and Amelia.

"Thank you, Papa," added Amelia.

"Well! I am sure no good will come of it." Mrs. Bertram shook her head, and looked grave. "But I can see your mind is quite made up, Mr. Bertram, so I will say no more about it."

CHAPTER 2

THE SOUND OF curtains being drawn back woke Viscountess Norland. Normally she would have grumbled at her abigail's lack of consideration, but today the disturbance was welcome. She had been dreaming she was back in the Bois de Bologne, staring down the barrel of de Livry's pistol in the pale, dawn light.

She massaged her shoulder. The scar still ached sometimes, when the weather was damp. "Good morning, Dorothea." She sat up and yawned. "Any news?"

"Rumours only." The plump woman thrust a folded newspaper at her and plonked the breakfast tray on the bedside table, slopping the hot chocolate over the rolls and kippers. Her lips were pressed tightly together.

"You are cross," observed Joanna. "With me?"

"No more than usual, your ladyship." Dorothea flounced over to the wardrobe and took out the green evening dress Joanna had worn last night—she had thought it best not to court scandal by wearing male attire the instant she was back in London. She tutted at the ripped seam, took it to the window seat, and reached for her sewing basket.

While Dorothea sewed, Joanna sipped her hot chocolate, buttered a roll and ate it, and picked at her kippers. Her hearty appetite of yesterday had deserted her, and she knew the reason why. She glanced at the newspaper then away again. She wasn't delaying reading the Gazette, she told herself, merely gathering her strength.

"It's not that I *mind* being poor," said Dorothea, after a moment. "Lord knows, that is nothing new. It's just that your ladyship said there would be no more wagering." She bit off the thread, discovered another ripped seam, and bent her head to her work once more.

"The Exchange isn't wagering." A pointed look told Joanna what Dorothea thought of *that* notion. "Well, perhaps it is. But I am certain my faith in the Duke will prove correct." As least, she hoped so.

It was no wonder Dorothea was vexed with her, she reflected ruefully. She was vexed with herself. What had yesterday seemed a racing certainty, after a good night's sleep felt like a very risky enterprise. Plunging herself in debt to a moneylender, buying up the shares that every sensible person was selling—the City was in a panic that Wellington's defeat was imminent . . . It would either make her or break her. She was no longer sure which.

"And to go to the Jews for the credit!" blurted her abigail. "They will hound us even on the Continent."

"Well, I could hardly approach Coutts or Drummond's." Joanna had grown tired of defending her actions. Dorothea was very dear to her but did occasionally overstep the mark. "What's done is done," she said shortly. "And for good or ill, I must live with the consequences."

"And so must I."

She chose to ignore her abigail's impertinence and instead turned her attention to the Gazette. "Are the rumours very bad?" When no reply was forthcoming, she took a deep breath, shook out the paper, and turned the pages to the despatch from Belgium.

The news, if such it could be called, was anything but reassuring. There had been actions at Ligny and Quatre-Bras—Boney had taken the Duke by surprise. Cavalry skirmishes at Genappe had followed. The Prussians were badly mauled, and there was even a rumour that Blücher had been killed. Her heart sank then she rallied herself. These were mere rumours.

She glanced at the still brooding Dorothea. "This morning's breakfast was a good deal better than yesterday's," she offered. "I take it you have now made friends with the servants?"

The furrowed brow smoothed a little. "Yes, your ladyship. I have the run of The George's kitchens." Dorothea sniffed. "Very provincial they are too, for all the owner's airs and graces."

Joanna smiled. "Did you spin your new friends a pretty yarn about our recent travels?"

An *affaire de coeur* had delayed Joanna from joining her countrymen in the headlong rout to the Channel, and Dorothea, faithful as always, would not leave her side. By the time Joanna *was* ready—she had parted from Marie easily enough in the end; perhaps her heart had not been engaged by the diminutive actress after all—

bribes were the order of the day, and the price of horses had become so exorbitant as to make them out of the question.

But she had always relished a challenge. They made their way from Paris cross-country, over fields and ditches, sleeping in barns and hayricks when no better accommodation was forthcoming, bypassing soldiers and roadblocks on the way. Such an adventure would have taxed most women to their limits, but they took it in their stride. Joanna's height and male attire, plus judicious use of her pistols, had kept trouble at bay, as had her almost perfect command of French.

Dorothea's gaze had become distant as she remembered, and now a smile curved her mouth. Joanna breathed a sigh of relief. Life was always much more congenial when her abigail was in a sunny mood.

"Cook opened her mouth so wide during the tale," said Dorothea, chuckling, "I was tempted to pop something in it." She set aside the evening dress, crossed to the basin and pitcher, and poured out some water for her mistress.

Joanna stretched the kinks from her shoulders. They had arrived back in England only two days ago, and she was still feeling the effects of her recent exertions. "It will be very pleasant to relax at my brother's house in the country."

Dorothea gave her a knowing glance. "You will be bored within a se'nnight."

"I shall not."

Joanna flung back the sheets and got out of bed. She stripped off her nightgown and began to wash herself. Dorothea folded the discarded garment and handed her a towel. While she dried herself, the abigail brought her underthings and walking dress to her.

"You will miss the attractions of a pretty face and a fine pair of eyes," predicted Dorothea.

Joanna pulled on her drawers and stockings. "You know me too well." She let herself be eased into a chemise and petticoat, demanded the stays be but lightly laced, and waited for Dorothea to button up the dress.

After that, the abigail turned her attention to Joanna's hair. Joanna preferred to leave her hair loose or tied back in a no nonsense queue, but Dorothea had other ideas. She swept back Joanna's hair into a bun then reached for the curling tongs that she had set to heat in the fire and tested them against a wet thumb. When they were ready, she set to work on the cluster of ringlets over each ear that was the latest fashion.

Joanna twiddled her thumbs, sang a saucy song she had learned from Marie—in the original French, but Dorothea still understood enough to tut loudly at some parts—and glanced at her abigail.

"Who is to say there will not be a pretty face and a fine pair of eyes at Thornbury Park? The women there can't *all* be antidotes."

Dorothea's lips thinned. "Think of your brother, your ladyship. To set the cat among the pigeons in his own back yard—"

"Is very tempting," interposed Joanna, unable to resist. She laughed at Dorothea's expression. "I was only teasing. I am not so inconsiderate a person as I once was." She felt a moment's doubt. "Am I?"

"No indeed." The abigail set aside the curling tongs and scrutinised her efforts. "There. All done." She gave Joanna's arm a reassuring pat and stood back.

Joanna checked her appearance in the mirror and nodded her thanks. "Well," she said, pulling on her half boots and donning the matching pelisse, hat, and kid gloves, "since we are confined to town until there is more definite news, and there is no point my sitting here with a fit of the dismals, I shall take the air. No doubt London has changed since I was last here. I shall investigate and report."

"As you wish, your ladyship," said Dorothea. "Dinner will be waiting for you when you return."

LONDON HAD INDEED changed in the five years Joanna had been away, both for the better and the worse. It smelled a great deal better than Paris, she decided, as she walked past St. Paul's and down Ludgate Hill; it was pleasant not to have to step over stinking gutters running with filth.

As she walked, she took the opportunity to eye the young ladies, both to admire their looks and appraise their clothes—*Parisiennes* wore their waists higher, their skirts wider. She glanced down at her scuffed half boots and faded pelisse. If her shares increased, she would buy new clothes—for herself and Dorothea. And hire a town coach to take her to Thornbury Park; it would be amusing to arrive in style. Then she would search for a place to rent. Would a town house or a country house be preferable? Perhaps Dorothea was right, and the country would be too stultifying. Perhaps she should first see how she fared at her brother's—

The bubble of her pleasant daydream burst. What if the shares she had so rashly bought plunged further?

Joanna began to strain her ears and eyes for news from across the Channel, eavesdropping on the conversations of passing gentlemen, who seemed disappointingly to be more concerned with Princess Caroline's latest *contretemps* with the Prince Regent than with the war. Her mood darkened, and she lowered her head and increased her pace, scarcely aware of where she was going, or of the contents of the Oxford Street shop windows.

She had promised Edmund she had mended her ways. What would he say if she turned up on his doorstep in hock up to her eyebrows?

A teashop appeared up ahead, and she became aware of just how weary she was and took refuge. She found a seat in a high-ceilinged room, crowded with chattering females who reminded her of a flock of twittering birds. This won't do, she admonished herself, ordering a pot of tea and some sandwiches. But disquieting thoughts kept returning, and in the end it seemed easier to think of nothing at all.

Somewhere a clock struck five, jarring Joanna out of a reverie, the details of which she could not recall. She was not far from Hyde Park, she realised. The fashionable hour had started half an hour ago. When she was younger, she had liked to watch the Ton as they paraded up and down. It would be a light-hearted distraction, and might lift her spirits.

A brisk walk soon brought her to Rotten Row, and she joined the convivial crowd of bystanders calling out to the elegant men and elaborately dressed women driving slowly up and down in their carriages.

She was laughing at a clipped poodle that had taken a severe dislike to a Dalmatian coach dog when a familiar voice said in her ear, "Well, well! If it isn't Notorious Norland. In a dress too, by God!"

She spun on her heel. "Perry!"

The first son of the Earl of Painswick raised his top hat and pressed her gloved fingers to his lips. Lord Peregrine looked up-to-the-minute as always—his green coat sported the latest M-notch collar. But he was less handsome than she remembered, the face below his delicately spiked fringe beginning to reflect his dissipation.

Nevertheless, she was delighted to see him. They had shared good times, the same interests, and on one occasion the favours of the same courtesan—a fact they only discovered later.

"I heard you were in Paris," he said.

"And I heard you were in Brighton." She eyed his extravagant neckcloth with amusement—it must be choking to wear such a thing, but Perry had always placed fashion above comfort.

"Insufferably dull place, Brighton."

Joanna gave him a knowing look. "You are out of funds, I take it?"

"Of course. For what is money for if not to spend it on the finer things in life?" He examined his yellow gloves. "In fact I am just off to tap my father for some more blunt."

"He hasn't cut you off then?"

"Not yet."

They were attracting attention, so Lord Peregrine gestured, and they began to walk. "Boney made things too hot for you over there, I collect."

"Yes. Would it also surprise you to know, I felt homesick?"

An eyebrow shot up.

"Truly. After all these years of travelling, I have been wondering if it is not time for me to settle down." She regarded him curiously. "Have you never felt that, Perry? A longing to set down roots somewhere, to have a place you can truly call 'home'?" Maybe she was getting old. She had never had such feelings before she turned thirty.

He waved a negligent hand. "Of course, m'dear Viscountess. But I take another drink, find myself another pretty wench, and the mood soon passes."

Joanna laughed. "You have not changed."

"Neither have you. Did I not find you here, ogling the ladies?"

"*Touché.*" They paused under a spreading chestnut tree. "I am staying at The George," she told him. "Come and dine with me."

He pretended to be horrified. "And risk incurring the disapproval of that abigail of yours?"

She laughed. "Deservedly so, I'm sure. But *I* am the one Dorothea currently disapproves off. For she is convinced I have made paupers of us."

His eyes twinkled. "Then I shall not trouble you for a loan."

"No indeed. But will you come?"

"I cannot, Joanna." His tone was regretful. "I have arranged to see my father, and am travelling down to Gloucestershire tonight."

She was sorry to hear that. Perry was a rogue, but he was entertaining company. "Well. And I shall likely be in Kent by the end of the week."

"At your brother's house?"

"Ay, at Thornbury Park."

"Then I daresay I shall visit you there and endeavour to alleviate your boredom." He pressed her hand to his lips once more and took his leave.

Joanna watched Lord Peregrine's elegant figure disappear into the distance, before turning and heading back to the Inn. There, under Dorothea's disapproving gaze, she picked half-heartedly at her lamb chop and potatoes, drank too much port, and fretted about the lack of news from Belgium.

It was a relief to retire for the night. But though she was exhausted, sleep was a long time coming. And when it finally arrived, it brought only nightmares in which great armies clashed, the tide of combat ebbed and flowed, and victory hung in the balance.

CHAPTER 3

IT WAS A glorious morning when Frederica and Amelia set off to walk the three miles to Thornbury Park. As they strolled, enjoying the late June sunshine and swinging their reticules, conversation kept returning to the glad tidings of two days ago.

The first sign something significant had happened was the ringing of church bells. Mr. Bertram had sent a footman down to the village to enquire about the peals. He had come running back to Chawleigh, red-faced and grinning, and bellowing to everyone and his dog that "the Duke of Wellington has defeated old Boney at Waterloo."

Everyone had cheered at the news, and a few of the servants had even danced a reel. It was as though a great weight had been lifted, and the weather obligingly mirrored the mood.

Halfway to their destination, though, and in the middle of Amelia's amusing anecdote at Herbert Smith's expense, the sun began to dim. Frederica glanced up at the swiftly gathering clouds in dismay.

"We must hurry," she urged her sister and quickened her pace accordingly. They had not gone many yards before the first drops of rain began to fall. "Perhaps it will be merely a shower." But it was a full-blown summer storm, and a few minutes later, they were running for cover, hair dripping, flimsy summer dresses plastered to their bodies.

As they cowered under an oak tree, thunder rumbled above them and lightning flashed. Amelia grew almost hysterical. Frederica's own nerves were badly shaken when a loud crack of lightning was followed by a broken branch thudding to earth a few feet from them. She embraced her sister and tried to comfort her, while she considered what to do. Amelia was trembling violently in her arms, whether from cold or fear she was unsure; Frederica herself felt uncomfortably chilled. They had passed the halfway point of their walk, or she would have advocated returning home. One thing was certain—they could not stay here under the oak tree. Another branch might fall.

She had just told her sister, "We must continue," and was urging her out into the rain once more, when movement caught her eye. A town coach was making its grand way along the road to Thornbury Park, its progress hampered by the driver having to coax horses made nervous by the storm.

She blinked the rain from her eyelashes and stared. "Amelia!" she cried.

"I see it."

"Wave. They must see us. They *must*."

She had begun to think neither the driver nor the coach's occupants had seen their frantic waving, when it began to slow. As it drew level with the oak tree, it halted, and the door opened.

A short woman, plump and with dark eyebrows, descended, and placed her feet gingerly on the wet ground. She drew her shawl over her head and picked her way across the grass towards them. When she was within hailing distance, she paused and shouted.

"Are you bound for Thornbury Park?" Her voice was barely audible above the elements.

Frederica thought it simplest to nod. A smile and a beckoning gesture were her reward. As the stranger turned and hurried back towards the coach, she urged her sister to follow. Moments later, they were climbing aboard and pulling the door closed behind them.

Almost at once, the coach lurched forward, tipping Frederica against her sister who objected with a squeal. She apologised, righted herself, and—at the plump woman's urging—accepted a rug for their knees and a shawl for their shoulders. At once she felt much warmer, and a sense of relief and gratitude overtook her.

"Oh thank you so much for stopping," she said, taking her sister's hands between hers and rubbing warmth into them. "It would have been very hard for us had you not." Ruefully she indicated her bedraggled state. "As you can see, the storm has got the better of us."

The woman smiled. "You can thank her ladyship not me." She indicated with her head, and it was only then that Frederica became aware there was another person sitting in the corner, gazing out of the window.

"Oh! I did not see you there." Belatedly she remembered her manners and blushed. "Thank you indeed," she addressed the silent figure. "My sister and I are both indebted to you."

The woman turned her head and nodded once before looking away once more. The coach's shadowy interior muted colours and merged shapes, making it difficult to see their mysterious benefactress. Frederica was left with an impression of a pale face and dark hair and that was all.

The loud clatter of rain on the roof lessened and died away, and they travelled on for a while in awkward silence.

"Frederica," whispered her sister at last, between chattering teeth. "Are we nearly there yet?"

As if in answer, the coach slowed and came to a halt. Then the door opened, and the Lyntons' footman was standing there, looking enquiringly up at them. His mouth gaped when he saw the bedraggled sisters.

"Is that you, Miss Bertram, Miss Amelia?"

"Indeed it is." Frederica glanced at the woman in the corner to see if it was permissible for them to disembark first and received a nod. "We got caught in the rain."

She let him help her down and waited while he did the same for Amelia. "Fortunately for us, her ladyship's coach—" *Ladyship*. It suddenly dawned on her just *whose* coach they had been riding in, and she struggled to maintain her composure. "Would you please tell Mr. Lynton that we are here to throw ourselves upon his mercy?"

"Very good, ma'am."

But there was no need for the footman to carry out that particular errand, because a startled, laughing, "My goodness! My sister has brought a couple of drowned rats with her," announced the presence of the master of the house himself, eliciting an uninhibited laugh from inside the coach.

"I do beg your pardon," he amended, catching Frederica's gaze and blushing. "That was unkind of me. You must be chilled to the bone." He turned towards the front porch and bellowed, "Caroline."

Seconds later his wife appeared, looking disapproving. "Good heavens, Edmund. I know your sister has arrived, but must you shout?"

Her gaze fell on Frederica and Amelia and her mouth dropped open. Once she collected her wits, though, she was sympathy itself. "Oh, you poor dears! Come in, come in. We must get you out of those wet things at once."

Edmund meanwhile was peering inside the coach. "What a splendid contraption. Is it yours or rented, Joanna?"

"Oh, rented, of course," came a female drawl.

The clouds had thinned, and the sun was threatening to appear once more. Frederica would have liked to stay to see the Viscountess alight and study her properly, but Amelia chose that moment to sneeze, which brought out the mother hen in Mrs. Lynton, and without further ado they were ushered inside.

"*THAT* WAS VISCOUNTESS Norland?" said Amelia. "How disappointing!" She stretched out her hands to the warmth. Caroline had ordered a fire lit in one of the many unused upstairs bedchambers.

"Indeed." Frederica gave her a sidelong glance. "You were expecting her to be dressed as a bandit and accompanied by a hideous hunchback, at the very least?"

Amelia snorted. Frederica was relieved to see that, now she was cosy and safe from danger, her sister's good humour had reasserted itself.

"No, I was not. Still. I wish we had been able to see more of her. Was she wearing men's clothes? I could not see, the coach was so gloomy. And she did not appear to be taking snuff."

"No, thank heavens. But no doubt we will have a better view of her on another occasion. Not, I think, today, though." From the other side of the door had come much shouting and the sounds of toing and froing—Edmund's servants helping their master's guest get settled into her new quarters.

Frederica pulled the towel closer around her shoulders and wiggled toes that were almost dry. Their wet clothes and shoes had been taken away, and Caroline was sorting out some of her own dresses for them to wear.

"That plump woman must be her maid," said Amelia. "Did you notice—her clothes were the latest thing; they looked brand new."

Frederica nodded. "The Viscountess must be trying to make a good impression on her brother. Her clothes are likely new too."

"And that coach. Have you ever *seen* anything so magnificent?"

"Only rented, I fear."

Amelia looked disappointed.

A knock at the door preceded Caroline's entrance. Their hostess had two morning dresses draped over her arm and two sets of matching shoes dangling from her hands. After a brief, rather heated, discussion about who should have the lavender or the pink, Amelia retired behind a screen to dress.

Frederica waited her turn patiently, grinning when her sister emerged. Amelia was rather more buxom than Caroline. The lavender dress was a tight fit on her, and the shoes pinched. The grin disappeared, however, when it was her turn, and not only did the shoes prove to be too large, the pink dress's waist was too low, its hem much too long. Not for the first time she wished she were a little taller. Still, rather too long a dress than too short, she decided, ignoring her sister's laughter and reassuring their apologetic hostess that she did not mind in the least about her outfit's shortcomings.

"You have been kindness itself, Mrs. Lynton. Please be easy. It is our own fault for not taking more notice of the weather before we set out."

"Well, if you are sure—"

"I am." Frederica regarded herself in the mirror and tried not to grimace. "Now, if a maid perhaps—" She gestured at her bedraggled locks. Caroline obligingly sent for Martha, her own maid.

When they were once more fit to be seen in civilised company, Caroline nodded her satisfaction, dismissed Martha, and said, "And now. Chaloner is waiting for you in the drawing room, Miss Bertram. And the children are in the schoolroom, eager as always to play with you, Miss Amelia." She put a hand on the door handle and waited.

"They are always such good-natured children," Amelia said, getting up and crossing to join the children's mother. Caroline looked doubtful.

"That's because you allow them to do whatever they have a mind to," said Frederica. She smoothed her unflattering dress over her hips, made a mental note to slide her feet rather than lift them—that way the shoes might stand some chance of staying on—and dismissed her dismal appearance from her mind.

Caroline smiled and opened the door. "Whatever the case, my three are always glad to see Miss Amelia. And I am happy to accommodate them."

"GOOD MORNING, MISS Bertram." Chaloner Dunster resumed his seat and smoothed the creases from his yellow nankeen trousers. "I trust you have taken no harm from your recent misadventure?"

Frederica made herself comfortable on the sofa while Caroline settled herself at the writing table in the drawing room window. "Good morning to you, Mr. Dunster. I am quite well, thank you. My clothes, however . . ." She gestured at her ill-fitting garments.

He blinked. "But are those not—"

"Your sister's?" She laughed and glanced across at their chaperone, who was already busy with her letter to her cousin. "Indeed they are. Either that, or I must find myself a new seamstress at once."

He looked puzzled, and she suppressed a sigh. Amiable, Chaloner might be; quick-witted, he was not.

"And your sister? I hope Miss Amelia has not caught a cold?"

Health was always a safe topic. "No, thank goodness. She is presently with the children." A shoe was sliding off her foot, and she retrieved it discreetly.

"Ah, my nephews and niece." Chaloner turned to smile in his sister's direction. "Caroline tells me she is always glad when 'Aunt' Amelia entertains them."

Since four-year-old George, five-year-old Maria, and six-year-old John were always exhausted and much more biddable after a visit from her energetic sister, it was no wonder, thought Frederica.

"And your family," he continued. "They are well too?" He flicked a speck of lint off his waistcoat.

"Indeed. We are *all* well at Chawleigh, Mr. Dunster." It was clearly up to her to change the topic of conversation. What would interest him, other than talk of his plans for Symond Hall, of which she had already heard far more than she would wish? "Is not the news from across the Channel wonderful? We were all loud in our huzzas when the footman brought the tidings."

"And now the Duke is marching on Paris," said Chaloner.

"So I hear. Let us hope he brings things to a swift conclusion."

He nodded.

"And that things soon return to normal. Cook is forever complaining about shortages of one foodstuff or another."

"Is she? I daresay the Lyntons' cook is the same." He turned to his sister. "Is she not, Caroline?"

"Oh, most certainly."

"I must hire a new cook for Symond Hall. The one who served my great uncle does not suit me at all. Her ideas are fifty years behind the times." He turned and smiled at Frederica. "But that decision should be made by the lady of the house, don't you agree?"

"To be sure. Or by the housekeeper." Frederica examined her hands, and an awkward silence fell. A rustle proved to be Caroline turning over her sheet of writing paper. Through the drawing room window, Frederica saw Viscountess Norland's hired coach and horses driving away—back to town, presumably.

"It was fortunate that the Viscountess saw us sheltering under the oak tree," she said.

Chaloner pursed his lips then nodded. It was clear he had little desire to talk about their notorious visitor, but Frederica found herself compelled to continue.

"She has just come from Paris, has she not?"

"Calais," corrected Caroline from the writing table. Her quill had broken, and she was sharpening a new point.

"Allow me." Chaloner rose and strode to his sister's side, then busied himself with a knife. The tip of his tongue poked out in concentration. Frederica turned her gaze away.

"According to Edmund," continued Caroline, "his sister left Paris a few weeks ago. She has been travelling overland, on foot."

Frederica looked up at this interesting titbit. "On foot! Then it is fortunate indeed that she came to no harm."

"Perhaps not so fortunate as all that."

Did Caroline wish her sister-in-law had not returned safely? wondered Frederica. Or did she mean that, where the Viscountess was concerned, fortune had little to do with her fate?

But Chaloner had returned to his seat opposite and was frowning at her. Recollecting herself, she gave him a charming smile.

His expression relaxed. "Have you heard, Miss Bertram? There is to be a ball at the assembly rooms in three weeks time."

Frederica nodded. "Amelia is all agog at the news and has been making our lives a misery trying to decide what to wear."

He laughed. "Miss Amelia enjoys her dancing, I hear. And you are not averse to it, I hope?"

"No indeed." Though it very much depended on one's dance partner, she reflected.

"Then perhaps you will keep the first few dances on your card free for me, Miss Bertram?"

She regarded him from under lowered eyelashes. Her parents would be delighted with the way matters were progressing. Did it necessarily matter that she felt nothing for him at all?

"Perhaps I shall."

CHAPTER 4

THE RED BALL rocketed into the corner pocket with a satisfying *clunk*.

"Three points," cried Joanna, throwing her brother a glance over her shoulder.

Edmund's wife, who was standing next to him, looked wide-eyed, and Joanna's heart sank. She had only been at Thornbury Park a week, but she seemed constantly to be offending the Dunster siblings' finer feelings.

"You should have used the cue rest, Joanna." Twinkling blue eyes belied her brother's reproving tone. "It is not considered decent for a lady," he stressed the word slightly, "to sprawl all over the billiard table."

She pushed herself upright and retrieved the ball from the table pocket. What shot should she try next? A cannon? "I didn't reveal anything I ought not to, Edmund, thanks to these." She patted a breech-clad thigh. She had been riding this morning—astride, much to Chaloner Dunster's disgust—and had opted not to change out of her riding outfit, which would usually have caused little comment except that Joanna preferred male attire.

She bent over the table's edge, sighted along the cue, and made her shot, striking first Edmund's cue ball then the red ball. "Two points."

"It is always unequal playing billiards with you," he complained.

She flashed him a grin and lined up her next shot. "We could play something else. Piquet?"

"You always win."

"We could go shooting instead?"

" 'Tis out of season. And my clay pigeon shooting is not up to your standard, I fancy."

The red ball clunked into the pocket again.

"You used not to be such a poor sport, Edmund."

"And you used not to be such a good one."

Joanna laughed and brushed a speck of dirt off the leather tip of her cue.

Things had at first been tense between them, but they had soon fallen back into their easy ways, resuming the banter of childhood. Of course, things weren't quite as they had been. Edmund now had a wife and three children—so far, Joanna had succeeded in staying out of the little horrors' way. As for his wife . . .

Caroline was, at least, trying to make allowances. It was clear her sister-in-law *wanted* to like Joanna, if only for her husband's sake, but she was wary, perhaps expecting Joanna to lapse into scandal and in the process hurt Edmund. It was understandable. The only way to convince Caroline of her sincerity was to persist. Caroline's brother, however . . . Well, sometimes Chaloner Dunster could do with a swift kick up the rear. And Joanna was currently wearing just the riding boots for the job.

Clunk. "Two points."

Thinking of Chaloner put her in mind of Miss Bertram, who was wont to visit him once or twice a week. It had become a favourite pastime with Joanna to spot the small, fair-headed figure walking briskly towards Thornbury Park with her sister in tow. Amelia was the younger and prettier of the two, but also, by all accounts, the more empty-headed. It was Miss Bertram herself who interested Joanna, though she could not have said why.

When she had first seen Frederica, much bedraggled and shepherding her hysterical sister into the coach, Joanna had not taken much notice of her, other than to admire her figure and the way her wet muslin clung to it. Now, she found herself scanning the estate for signs of the young woman and passing the time conjecturing about her circumstances and attitudes.

For example. Did the fact that Frederica wore the same walking dress on each occasion indicate poverty, frugality, or pragmatism? Was the simple, slightly dated style her own choice or one imposed on her by others? And why, at twenty-seven, had she not married—was she too choosy, bad-tempered, or was it simply a lack of suitors?

Joanna potted the red ball. "Three points."

Not that Miss Bertram lacked suitors any more apparently. Chaloner had high hopes in that direction, Edmund had confided.

Frederica would be wasted on that dullard, she decided. He would do better to look to her sister.

She fluffed her next shot on purpose, and Edmund grunted, "At last!" and took his turn at the table.

Joanna leaned her hip against the wall, ostensibly watching her brother but really wondering what was for lunch.

Her appetite had returned, and she felt much less tired than she had. Maybe it was the country air, or simply being able to relax at last. Or maybe it was the luxurious bed—she hadn't slept so well or so long in ages. Or woken so spryly. Going to bed sober might have something to do with that, of course. Why, this morning Dorothea had even commented about the lack of dark circles around Joanna's eyes. Perhaps she had been looking as dissipated as Perry and never realised it.

Ivory balls clacked together, and Edmund murmured, "Two points."

"Well done, my dear." Caroline clapped her hands.

Joanna smiled and turned her gaze out of the window. Edmund's country house was beautifully situated. One thousand rolling acres of grass, woodland, and farmland stretched in all directions, and she had yet to explore it all on horseback.

"Is Miss Bertram due to come this afternoon?" she asked idly.

"Oh dear!" Caroline's exclamation made Joanna look round. "I had forgotten all about her. I arranged to visit Mrs. Penson and take her some of cook's delicious beef broth." Joanna had early on learned that Edmund's wife was as concerned for the welfare of the estate workers as her husband. "She has been quite poorly you know."

Joanna leaned on her cue. "Why is that a difficulty?"

Her sister-in-law shot her an exasperated glance. "Miss Bertram cannot possibly meet my brother unchaperoned. He would not countenance it." She looked at her husband. "Is that not so, Edmund?"

"Indeed it is. Chaloner has very decided views on the matter." He leaned over the billiard table and took another shot.

"Then leave the door open," suggested Joanna.

"That will not do either," said Edmund. "But there *is* another solution to hand. Joanna can take your place, Caroline."

"Indeed she cannot!" His wife's cheeks reddened. "I beg your pardon, Joanna. I did not mean . . ."

"Please, do not apologise," said Joanna, hoping she didn't sound as nettled as she felt. It was one thing for *her* to object to the idea, quite another for her brother's wife. "I understand completely. My reputation is hardly conducive to such a respectable role."

Caroline looked relieved to be so quickly understood.

"Nevertheless," continued Joanna, driven by some devilish impulse, "I am female, married, and over thirty. And are not those the primary requirements for the post?" Belatedly, it occurred to her that she was talking herself into a corner.

"Indeed." Edmund straightened, cue in one hand, and regarded his wife. "And if my sister is willing to help us out of this little difficulty, my dear, it is churlish to refuse."

Caroline flushed a darker shade. "But Chaloner—"

"Is a guest in my house," he reminded her. "He will respect my opinion on this matter."

Seeing her plans for a brisk ride after lunch disappearing rapidly, Joanna added, "But we must surely heed your wife's feelings on the matter, Edmund. A trusted female servant would do as well. Failing that, it is the simplest matter to despatch a footman to Chawleigh House with a message . . ." She trailed off as Edmund turned towards her, blue eyes knowing.

"It will not be so hard for you to spend half an hour quietly in the drawing room, Joanna. You have a book to read, do you not?" He raised an eyebrow.

Joanna ground her teeth but nodded. She had indeed, and now regretted telling him as much.

"You are determined to turn me respectable," she murmured, as she brushed past her brother to take her turn at billiards.

"And you will of course," said Edmund, smiling, "wear more suitable clothing."

Joanna resisted the urge to brain him with her cue.

THE OPENING OF the drawing room door roused Joanna. She marked her place with her finger and looked up. "Good afternoon, Mr. Dunster."

Chaloner's lips thinned. "Good afternoon."

He had omitted her title, and his tone was barely civil, but she ignored the slight. After all, a respectable chaperone—a notion that still made her smirk inwardly—could afford to, surely?

Edmund had left that morning's Gazette lying on a chair, and his sour-faced brother-in-law grabbed it, sat down, and hid himself behind it, turning the pages noisily.

Joanna shook her head at his childish antics and returned to her reading—the latest novel by the anonymous author of *Waverley*.

Dorothea had recommended it. "It should have action and romance enough to suit even your ladyship's lurid tastes," she'd said, before tut-tutting at the muddy state of Joanna's boots and whisking them away for cleaning.

So far, her abigail had been right. The book's young hero—whose surname, oddly enough, was the same as Frederica's—had been kidnapped by smugglers and taken to Holland. It looked as if he was going to India next. Strange place, India. Exotic and colourful, hot and dirty and dangerous. She had preferred Greece.

The clock on the mantelpiece began to chime the half-hour. Simultaneously, Chaloner folded his newspaper and the door opened.

Miss Bertram stood framed in the doorway. Her gaze took in the room and its occupants, halting when it arrived at Joanna's seat by the window. Green eyes widened, and soft lips parted before closing again.

"Good afternoon, your ladyship. I was expecting Mrs. Lynton."

"Unfortunately, my sister had a pressing engagement elsewhere, Miss Bertram," said Chaloner, before Joanna could reply. "Edmund proposed his sister as replacement."

He had risen swiftly to his feet, and now advanced towards Frederica, taking her gloved hand, a gesture that took the young woman aback if her heightened colour was any indication. She let him lead her to a seat, where she smoothed her walking dress—the same one as always—and regained her aplomb.

Joanna nodded acknowledgement of Frederica's greeting, then wrenched her gaze back to the pages of her book. For some reason *Guy Mannering* seemed duller than it had.

She found herself eavesdropping on the murmur of conversation going on a few feet from her. Not that it amounted to much. So far, Chaloner had discussed the weather—the sunny afternoon made Joanna long to be outside—and asked after the health of every single member of Frederica's family, including the servants.

She tried not to roll her eyes. If these two were destined for marriage, as everyone seemed so certain they were, they had leaped over young lovers courting and gone straight into old married couple. She had never seen a pair so ill-suited, or so lacking in that vital spark.

The words on the page in front of her failed to register. Instead, she became aware that Frederica and Chaloner, independently of one another, kept darting covert glances in her direction. It dawned on her that her presence was affecting the couple in a way that Caroline's presumably did not. Edmund had not foreseen that.

The health of all parties successfully negotiated, an awkward pause ensued. It was Frederica who broke it.

"And how is Symond Hall progressing?"

Joanna hid a grimace. Chaloner had talked at length to all and sundry at Thornbury Park on that particular subject, to the point where even his sister had grown weary of it. Frederica's conversational gambit had the effect she no doubt intended, though, and Chaloner brightened considerably and began to talk.

"Oh, very well, Miss Bertram. Could not be better, in fact. The workmen have refurbished the dining parlour, conservatory, and library. To my specifications exactly, they assure me." He went on at length, cataloguing what had been knocked down and rebuilt, the precise shade of the curtains, and the exact width of stripe on the fashionable wallpaper. Joanna thought Frederica's eyes became slightly glazed, though from this distance it was hard to tell.

"It will be considerably different than it was in my great uncle's day," concluded Chaloner at last, leaning forward in his seat. "Do you like the Chinese style, Miss Bertram?"

In Joanna's opinion, the chinoisery affected by the Prince Regent was best confined to his Marine Pavilion in Brighton, and ill-suited for a gentleman's country house. She listened with interest to Frederica's reply.

There was a long pause. The answer, when it came, was a masterpiece of diplomacy and evasion. Although Frederica seemed of Joanna's opinion, her reply was also enough to satisfy Chaloner. Joanna silently applauded.

"Of course, the lady of Symond Hall, when there is one," he gave his fair companion a complacent, slightly knowing look, "will be able to add her own touches to the décor, should she wish."

Joanna realised she had read the same sentence ten times and was still none the wiser. She turned the page, the slight rustle attracting attention, which she pretended not to notice. She was relieved when the couple looked away again.

A glance at the clock showed that, though it had felt like a week, only ten minutes had passed. She thought wistfully of the riding she was missing.

Another pause was followed by Frederica asking about Caroline's pressing engagement.

"My sister is visiting Mrs. Penson," Chaloner informed her. "She has been poorly, as I think she mentioned to you on a previous occasion. Caroline is the soul of kindness. She is also acutely aware of the duties and obligations that her position as Edmund's wife entails."

Joanna could almost feel his gaze burning into her. He was playing a new game, she sensed. Superficially, his comments might be addressed to Frederica, but they were aimed at her and at her expense.

"Indeed," said Frederica. "She has always been generosity itself to my sister and myself."

"As have your family to her. Miss Amelia is such a help with the children, is she not?"

"But that is no hardship. For she enjoys playing with them."

"Nevertheless, such conduct is exemplary. A woman's interests should always centre around her children and home, do you not agree?"

Joanna resisted the urge to say something rude. Frederica uttered some noncommittal remark and deftly changed the subject. Soon the couple were discussing next week's ball.

"And will any of your friends be going?" asked Frederica.

"Alas, no, Miss Bertram," returned Chaloner. "I had hoped a friend might be able to come, but he declined. Too busy in town, he said, but I think the truth is he dislikes dancing."

Frederica laughed, and Joanna's ears pricked up at the welcome sound. "Not all men like balls. My father has always preferred to stay by the fire, with a cigar, a glass of brandy, and a good book."

Chaloner smiled. "Good is the operative word. A book should improve the mind. So many of today's ills arise from women reading unsuitable literature." He glanced meaningfully at Joanna.

"Though I am inclined to agree with you in the case of Mrs. Radcliffe's novels," said Frederica, for the first time sounding annoyed, "you are too harsh on my sex, Mr. Dunster. Are we allowed no respite from our daily lives, no escape, even for a moment?"

His barb had clearly hit an unintended target, and he flushed. "I beg your pardon, Miss Bertram." Joanna smirked as he struggled to backtrack. "I do not include you in my strictures, of course."

"Thank you."

After that, the conversation circled around less controversial topics, such as the attractions of Bath (which Joanna had always thought unutterably dull; she preferred Paris and the theatre—that was where she had met Marie) and when they had last visited there.

At last, the clock on the mantelpiece began to chime the hour. As the other occupants of the drawing room rose to their feet, Joanna did likewise, resisting the urge to stretch the cramp from her limbs. A good gallop was what she needed, to blow the cobwebs away.

She followed them to the door. There, Frederica's gaze dropped to the title of the book she carried before lifting to scrutinise her face. Joanna raised an eyebrow in query, and found herself on the receiving end of a rueful smile, which she felt compelled to return. The smile had transformed Frederica's face into something altogether charming. All too soon, the moment was over, though, and the young woman was turning away, taking her leave of them both.

When Frederica had gone up to the schoolroom in search of her sister, Chaloner threw Joanna a disgusted glance and strode off towards his own chamber.

"So glad I could be of assistance, Mr. Dunster," she called after him. "No imposition at all." He didn't deign to reply, but turned the corner out of sight. She shook her head at his behaviour. "'Pon my word! The man's a clodpole."

Back in her own chambers, she found that Dorothea, prescient as always, had laid out her clean boots and her riding wear. She donned the skin-tight breeches, single-breasted waistcoat, and double-breasted coat quickly, and headed for the stables.

CHAPTER 5

AFTER THE DAPPLED gloom of the woods, the sunlight was dazzling. Frederica glanced at her sister as they emerged into the open. "Put on your bonnet, Amelia. The sun is too fierce."

Amelia was enjoying the warmth, and merely twirled her bonnet by its ribbons. Frederica sighed and shook her head.

They continued on, taking the path that led towards the Lyntons' hay meadow. Amelia had expressed a wish to see how the labourers were progressing, and Frederica had happily agreed.

Three days ago, they had stopped to watch the teams of men moving in lines down the meadow. The easy rhythm of the scythes as they cut the grass and broad-leaved clover close to the ground was almost hypnotic. Every hand was needed when it came to gathering in the winter fodder, and behind the red-faced men had come women and children, the latter laughing and darting about like swallows as they helped turn the freshly cut grass so it would dry more evenly.

Sometimes, Edmund Lynton himself worked alongside his labourers, apparently, but there had been no sign of him on Monday. This year at least, thought Frederica, regarding with pleasure the countryside she loved so much, the weather would not ruin the crop—June was determined to show July its sunniest face.

"They are there." Amelia started forward. "Look."

There were indeed signs of activity in the meadow up ahead, but a heat haze distorted the view. As they drew closer, though, Frederica could make out the rosy cheeks of the sweating labourers, as they pitched forkfuls of dried grass up onto the carts, and the brown of weathered faces and forearms.

Amelia stopped by the fence, her presence earning her smiles and tugged forelocks. She seemed content for it to be so.

"Your bonnet," reminded Frederica; the sun was beating down, and there was no shelter.

Grumbling under her breath, her sister put it on and tied the ribbons under her chin, then resumed her scrutiny of the bustling meadow. "Oh! Is that not Edmund?"

Frederica followed Amelia's pointing finger. A labourer wielding a pitchfork, a gentleman by his clothes, was tossing the grass up onto a cart. "I do believe it is." Edmund had discarded his coat and neckcloth and rolled up his shirtsleeves.

She squinted at the figure receiving the hay on top of the cart, who was also wearing gentleman's clothing. There was something familiar about him.

"Who is that?" wondered Amelia.

The man's long black hair was gathered in a queue to keep it out of his face. But there was something about the way the damp shirt clung to him, and the full hips shown to advantage by snug-fitting, beige cloth trousers.

"Good lord!" Frederica put a hand to her mouth. "I do believe it's the Viscountess."

Amelia regarded her as though she had taken leave of her senses. "How can that be?" Then she looked again, and her mouth dropped open. "But she is wielding a pitchfork like the men! And look at what she is wearing." Her cheeks flushed. "Outrageous! We should retreat at once, Frederica. Before they notice us."

At that moment, Edmund caught sight of the two sisters. His face broke into a smile, and he threw down his pitchfork and strode towards them. As he walked, he yelled something over his shoulder, and the figure on top of the cart straightened then leaped to the ground with easy grace and followed him.

"Too late," said Amelia.

"Miss Bertram, Miss Amelia," panted Edmund, as he leaned on the fence. "Have you come to watch us haymaking?" He pulled out a red kerchief and mopped sweat and dust from his brow. "It is hard work, as you can see, but we were short-handed. I hope you will not think the less of me."

"No indeed, Mr. Lynton," said Frederica. "Rather the reverse. For the hay must be got in before the weather changes, must it not?"

"It must indeed."

Though she was speaking to Edmund, Frederica's gaze kept returning to the person coming up behind him. Viscountess Norland had grass seeds in her hair and dirt on her face. Her shirtsleeves were ripped and her trousers dusty and grass-stained, but she seemed unconcerned about her appearance.

She realised she was staring and regarded her hands while she composed herself. "Your ladyship."

"Good morning, Miss Bertram, Miss Amelia. I trust you are both well? My brother has me earning my keep, as you see." The Viscountess wiped her face on her sleeve, redistributing the dirt, then smiled, her teeth brilliant against the grime. She looked like a street urchin.

Frederica found herself unable to resist that radiant smile. "Indeed. It is a fine morning for haymaking, is it not?"

"Too hot for my liking," said Edmund.

Viscountess Norland gave him a wry glance. "Hot? You should try living in Greece, brother."

"I think not."

Amelia was still staring at the Viscountess's clothes, and Frederica kicked her unobtrusively on the ankle. She hissed in startlement and plastered a stiff smile on her face. The Viscountess gave her a curious glance but returned her attention to Frederica.

Her eyes were quite striking, observed Frederica—a much paler shade of blue than her brother's. And they were looking right back at her. A dark eyebrow rose in query, and she flushed and searched for something to say.

"Your brother pressed you into his service, your ladyship?"

"Now there you are quite wrong, Miss Bertram. Foolishly, I volunteered for this penal servitude." The fond glance she gave Edmund took the sting from her words. "It was this or kick up my heels at Thornbury Park. I am easily bored, I'm afraid, and must take plenty of exercise. It is a sad flaw in my character, is it not, Edmund?"

"Most certainly."

The Viscountess threw her brother a look of mock outrage, and Frederica stifled a smile.

Amelia stood silent beside her. It was up to Frederica to keep the conversation flowing. "Ah. Then you have finished your book?" she enquired.

The Viscountess nodded and was about to reply when one of the labourers, a grey-bearded old man in a worn smock, approached, and to Frederica's amazement called out, "Beggin' your pardon, your ladyship, but we need you back on the cart."

Far from appearing annoyed, the Viscountess gave the man a friendly wave and yelled back, "In that case I will come at once, Ned."

She turned back to them. "If you'll excuse me, Miss Bertram, Miss Amelia. The foreman calls, and I must go." And go she did, haring back towards the cart and vaulting up on top of it with the ease of a gazelle. There, she proceeded to receive a pitchfork of dried grass and start distributing it evenly.

Edmund glanced at his sister. "Ay, and I must go too, or I'll never hear the end of it." His smile was rueful. "Ned has worked this meadow since he was a lad," he explained. "I defer to him in all matters concerning it. Good morning to you, ladies. Enjoy the rest of your walk."

The Bertram sisters watched their neighbour pick up the pitchfork he had dropped, then exchanged glances and started the journey home.

"Well!" said Amelia, as they walked. "That was very queer."

"Mm."

For a while they walked in thoughtful silence.

"It is indeed ironic," observed Frederica eventually, "that the only one of our acquaintance entitled to call herself 'ladyship' should care so little for ladylike conduct." She was torn between disapproval and admiration. She knew she should be shocked, but instead she felt oddly thrilled by the Viscountess's behaviour. And her appearance had been so singular.

Chawleigh House came into sight, and they walked briskly towards it.

"Whatever will Mama say when we tell her?" asked Amelia.

Frederica gave a mock-shudder. "I cannot imagine." But she could, all too well, and in the event, she was proved right.

"Shocking! Disgraceful behaviour, Mr. Bertram! And our two girls witness to such a thing. You must do something about that woman. At once."

"Do what, my dear?" He turned the pages of his newspaper. "Tell her that you disapprove? I hardly think *that* will change the Viscountess's ways."

"I suppose next you'll be advocating that our own daughters borrow their brothers' clothes and go haymaking with the villagers."

He pursed his lips in apparent consideration. "Frederica. What do you think? Are you eager to try your hand at haymaking?"

She knew from the twinkle in his eyes that he did not mean the question seriously. "No, Papa. Walking is quite sufficient exercise for me."

Beside her on the drawing room sofa, Amelia nodded. "I do not think I would make a good haymaker."

"You see, Mrs. Bertram. While it may suit the Viscountess, such activities would not suit either of our girls, so you must put such schemes out of your head." He turned back to his newspaper.

Their mother gave him an uncertain look. "I was not suggesting . . . How can you possibly . . ." She frowned and for a moment was silent, then she returned to her original topic. "A Viscountess should have more respect for her position. Has she not considered the unsettling effect of her behaviour on the villagers? Why, before we know it—"

"Perhaps it has not occurred to you, my dear," Mr. Bertram interrupted his wife, "but it has certainly occurred to me. If the Viscountess is helping her brother bring in his hay, and occasionally acting as chaperone when Mrs. Lynton is unavailable, then she has far less time to spend on scandalous pursuits. Now, tell me, Mrs. Bertram? Is that not in fact a blessing in disguise?"

"I . . . You . . ."

As their mother lapsed into frustrated silence, Frederica and Amelia exchanged glances—Frederica's amused, Amelia's thoughtful.

"Peace and quiet at last," muttered their father. "Now perhaps I may read."

FREDERICA SET OFF alone to walk the three miles to Thornbury Park. Amelia had pleaded a sick headache. Whether it was the result of leaving off her bonnet yesterday, or a wish on her sister's part to avoid seeing the Viscountess so soon after their rather startling encounter in the hay meadow, Frederica was unsure—she had not enquired too deeply.

She was glad to be alone for once. Amelia tended to prattle, about the rapidly approaching ball, or the magnificent figure Lt. so-and-so cut in his uniform, or her latest trial with poor, boring Mr. Smith. She was profoundly glad to be able to walk at her own pace, enjoying the sunshine and the surrounding countryside, and listening to the musical trill of a blackbird.

As Thornbury Park came into view, though, her spirits lowered. A trial of her own lay ahead. Chaloner Dunster was close to proposing, she was sure of it. His manner towards her had changed markedly since that awkward occasion when Viscountess Norland had acted as their chaperone.

He had taken to smiling fondly at her. He also insisted on complimenting her constantly, remarking on each and every little thing. He had admired the fineness of her eyes, the length of her eyelashes, the nobleness of her profile, the height of her forehead, the fullness of her lips, and slenderness of her ankles. He approved the sensible cut of her clothes and applauded her love of walking. Her opinions were astute for a woman, her sentiments a credit to her sex. And each time she must thank him, of course. It was becoming tedious.

At first she had felt flattered, then she saw beyond the smile and honeyed words and sensed he was doing and saying such things because it was expected of him. But who was she to judge his actions? Was she not as false?

Frederica rang the doorbell, and a footman appeared and showed her into the drawing room. The displeasure on Chaloner's face when he saw her took her aback, before she realised its true cause. The Viscountess was sitting by the window, quill in hand.

"Good afternoon, Mr. Dunster. Your ladyship."

The dark-haired woman nodded a greeting and returned to her writing. She was wearing more conventional attire, today, noted Frederica, suppressing a smile at the thought of what Chaloner must have made of yesterday's outfit.

Assuming a winning smile, he rose to his feet. "Miss Bertram. As always, it is delightful to see you." He captured her gloved hand and led her to a seat.

"My sister was called away once more. I fear Mrs. Penson has taken a turn for the worse."

"I am very sorry to hear that, Mr. Dunster."

The conversation started out as it always did, with observations about the weather and enquiries after the health of their various relatives, Chaloner expressing concern for Amelia's sick headache before forgetting all about her.

Frederica threw him a number of conversational sops, including a mention of Symond Hall, but he didn't take them. He seemed more inclined to make barbed comments at his sister-in-law's expense. It was an unpleasant side to his character of which she had been unaware prior to Viscountess Norland's arrival. It took all her self-control not to snap at him and much steering of the conversation into more tactful waters.

If he had planned to make his declaration, he clearly felt unable to do so in the presence of the Viscountess. Relief surged through Frederica, followed by a wave of guilt and depression. It was only putting off the inevitable.

In spite of her best efforts, she found her gaze straying often towards the quiet figure at the writing table, who was sometimes writing, sometimes staring out of the window, and on one occasion sucking the end of her quill. For the umpteenth time, she dragged her eyes away and tried to listen, without grinding her teeth, to the decided opinions of the man she would probably marry.

At last, the clock on the mantel chimed the hour, releasing her from purgatory.

She lost no time in setting off to walk back to Chawleigh, but had gone only a few yards when the sound of running footsteps and a shouted, "Miss Bertram," made her pause and turn round. Viscountess Norland was hurrying towards her.

She scanned her surroundings. There was no one else near—she was indeed the Viscountess's target. Her heart began to race. "Your ladyship?"

"I see you are alone today, Miss Bertram. May I walk with you?"

"That . . . would be pleasant," said Frederica politely if not exactly truthfully.

Blue eyes examined her. "Ah, but you are merely being kind. I do not wish to intrude. Enjoy your walk, Miss Bertram." The Viscountess turned away.

"Wait." This unexpected show of consideration had quite disarmed Frederica. Chaloner would not have been so thoughtful, she felt sure. "Please. Walk with me."

The Viscountess hesitated then nodded and fell into step beside Frederica. "Thank you."

They strolled a few paces in silence. Frederica's heart had returned to its normal rhythm, and she was beginning to relax when the Viscountess observed, "The last half hour must have been very dull for you, Miss Bertram. My fault, I fear. My presence seems to irk Mr. Dunster. But it could not be helped. Caroline was called away at short notice and would go."

Frederica wondered if her cheeks were as red as they felt. Viscountess Norland was nothing if not direct, she was fast discovering. She felt an urge to reply in kind and gave in to it. "Dull for you too, your ladyship."

An unladylike snort took her aback. "All this 'your ladyship' this, 'your ladyship' that, Miss Bertram. It is long-winded. Joanna is my name." She gave Frederica an expectant look.

Frederica blinked. "You wish me to call you by your name?"

"Rather that than by one of the many soubriquets, unrepeatable in polite company, by which I am known." The Viscountess smiled.

"Oh!" She flushed. "Then, Joanna, please, call me Frederica."

Joanna nodded. "Much better, Frederica."

They walked on in silence once more, Frederica musing on the odd twist of fate that had led her to be on first name terms with a Viscountess. Then she remembered her manners and cast around for something to talk about.

"You have finished your book?"

"Ah yes, we were interrupted when last you asked," said Joanna, glancing at her. "I have. And Dorothea has reclaimed it from me. And rapped my knuckles soundly for dog-earing the pages into the bargain."

Frederica blinked. "Dorothea?"

"My abigail. You met her."

"I did?"

"In the coach the day of the storm. Plump. Thick eyebrows."

Frederica restrained herself to a muffled, "Ah."

"You are surprised I read my abigail's books and allow her to chide me."

She was, but she was also reluctant to admit it.

"Dorothea has been with me over ten years and takes a great many liberties," said the Viscountess placidly. "She is also a friend and knows my taste in literature, and a great many other things."

Frederica was sure her eyes must be bulging. "Ah," she repeated.

"I do not read a great deal as a rule," continued Viscountess Norland. "I lack application, so Dorothea informs me. But you read, I think, do you not, Frederica?"

Relieved that the conversation was heading for safer ground, she nodded.

"Do you have a favourite author?" prompted her companion.

"Oh. Pardon me, your . . . Joanna. Yes. Though I do not know her name. She is the anonymous author of such works as *Sense and Sensibility* and *Pride and Prejudice*."

The Viscountess looked thoughtful. "I have heard of them. Would you recommend them to me?"

Frederica felt her cheeks warming. How to reply? "I do not think so, Joanna," she said carefully. "They are wonderfully well done novels of their kind, and I very much enjoyed them, but the author herself admits that she paints 'little pieces of ivory.' If I do not miss my guess, you would prefer something more," she searched for the word, "colourful. Sweeping vistas rather than dainty miniatures."

Her fear she might have offended the Viscountess proved groundless when the other woman threw back her head in a delighted guffaw. "Colourful, eh? You may be right, Frederica. I do like my books to have plenty of action in them. A duel, smugglers, pirates, pretty damsels in distress. Gallons of blood at the very least."

Frederica was uncertain if she was being teased, so she restricted herself to an enigmatic smile. Joanna returned the expression in kind.

They reached the oak tree where she and Amelia had taken shelter from the storm. The Viscountess looked at it then at Frederica.

"Your sister has a less robust constitution than you, I think?"

She considered. "I do not think so, but she is more careless of her health."

"She is very young. Only twenty still, I gather?"

"Nineteen," corrected Frederica.

"At that age many are careless, and some are very foolish indeed. Fortunately, with age comes wisdom. If we are lucky to survive so long." Her gaze seemed far away, and Frederica wondered if she was speaking of herself.

"You talk like a crone," she said lightly, "instead of a woman of one-and-thirty."

Joanna laughed and bobbed a mock curtsey. "Why, thank you. Such wisdom coming from a youngster of seven-and-twenty."

Frederica was startled that the Viscountess should know her exact age. But, very likely, conversation at Thornbury Park turned occasionally to the subject of herself and her sister. It would be unusual if the Viscountess had *not* heard details from her brother and her sister-in-law.

She realised she was finding the Viscountess's company surprisingly congenial, for all it was disconcerting. Much more congenial than Chaloner's. Though the conversation did occasionally verge on the improper, she felt easy with her. She wondered if this indicated a flaw in her own character, a want of morals perhaps. She wished she could talk to someone about it, but there was only her father, and somehow she didn't think—

"You are far, far away, Frederica."

Awareness of her surroundings came back with a rush. "I beg your pardon, your ladyship. I did not mean—"

"And we are back to 'your ladyship.'" The tone was frosty.

Frederica's cheeks warmed. "Joanna." She regarded Joanna intently and relaxed. "But you are teasing me."

"I am," agreed the Viscountess, giving her a brilliant smile.

They resumed their walk, and Frederica cast a sidelong glance at Joanna. "Is it true you once fought a duel?"

Joanna missed a step. "Yes, it is true."

Her eyes widened. She had imagined it to be exaggeration.

"I took a bullet for my pains." The Viscountess indicated her right shoulder with a gloved hand. "It was a year ago, in Paris. The wound still aches when the weather is damp."

"And your opponent?"

"De Livry? Dead as a doornail."

For a few paces, there was a sombre silence.

"Did he deserve it?" asked Frederica at last.

"Yes." Joanna gave her a rueful smile. "But I would say that, would I not?"

She had remained close-mouthed on the cause of the duel, noted Frederica. Disappointed, she confined herself to a neutral, "Indeed."

They walked on a few paces more.

"Have you ever visited Paris?" asked Joanna.

"Me? No."

"Have you never desired to go?"

"No. I am content to remain here." Frederica gestured at the countryside. "And why would I not be? Have you ever seen anything so beautiful as Kent?"

"Indeed, it is lovely." Joanna raised an eyebrow, an expression that was becoming familiar to Frederica. "But have you really never had a hankering to travel? Be honest now."

The glib reply died on Frederica's lips. "I daresay I did when I was younger," she admitted after a long silence. "But I knew travel was beyond my reach, Joanna, so I put it out of my head."

The Viscountess nodded, as though her answer had confirmed something. "You are a pragmatist. Determined to make the best of your circumstances, no matter how unpalatable they are. Is that the case with Mr. Dunster?"

The intimate question shocked Frederica. For a moment she was speechless. Then words returned. "How dare you judge me! You with your title and your wealth. How could someone like you possibly understand the dilemma that faces someone in my position?"

"I beg your pardon." Joanna was the picture of remorse. "That was tactless and impertinent of me, and I apologise." She reached for Frederica's hand, refusing all attempts to evade her. "Dorothea tells me that I have the manners of a barbarian, and I fear she is correct."

Frederica dropped her gaze, but Joanna ducked her head and peered up at her. The concern and sincerity in the Viscountess's eyes seemed genuine, and Frederica felt her anger fading as rapidly as it had arisen. The sensation of gloved fingers rubbing hers was distracting, as soothing as it was oddly stimulating, but she made no attempt to free herself. Her cheeks must be a brilliant red, she was sure.

"Please, forgive me and forget I ever raised the subject," continued the Viscountess, straightening when Frederica felt able to look her in the eye once more. "I would not have offended you for the world."

Fortunately for both, perhaps, the thudding of hoof beats drew their attention to something completely different. A rider was galloping along the road towards them on a bay thoroughbred, a dandy by the tightness of his breeches and the cut of his green coat.

The Viscountess rubbed Frederica's fingers one last time then released her hand. "Can it be?"

Frederica stared at the approaching rider. "Your brother is expecting a visitor?"

"He has come to see me, I fancy. That is an old friend of mine. Perry. Lord Peregrine."

A friend? Then why was there a touch of apprehension in the Viscountess's eyes? But as the rider drew near, Joanna's face broke into a smile, and she walked towards him.

As the thoroughbred thundered towards Joanna, Frederica's heart was in her mouth, but the Viscountess showed no fear. When the horse was almost upon her, the rider with the preposterously high collar and intricately tied neckcloth jerked sharply on the reins and pulled it to a halt a pace from her. She reached up and patted the horse's lathered neck then took off a glove and rubbed her hand over its nose.

"Who is this beauty?"

The horse lipped Joanna's hand.

"His name is Lightning." The man dismounted, his highly polished boots hitting the earth with a thump. "Apt, don't you think, Joanna? Got him yesterday. Couldn't resist putting him through his paces."

The new arrival's gaze fell on the silently watching Frederica, and he smiled. "But who is this charming article? Introduce me, do. Where are your manners, Joanna?"

Some would have found him charming, supposed Frederica. But she found his tone patronising. Something about this handsome stranger made her nape hairs bristle.

"This is our neighbour, Miss Bertram," said Joanna. "Miss Bertram, may I introduce Lord Peregrine, eldest son of the Earl of Painswick?"

"My lord." She curtseyed, and he bowed slightly in return.

"Miss Bertram."

"She is of no interest to you, Perry," continued the Viscountess, before he could speak. "She is spoken for."

Frederica blinked in astonishment at Joanna's bluntness, and became thoughtful. At her words, disgruntlement had flitted across his face, but Lord Peregrine was once more all smiling charm.

"I have been escorting Miss Bertram home." Joanna turned towards Frederica, her gaze solicitous. "You are more than halfway, Miss Bertram. Will you be content to continue the rest of the way alone?"

The return to a formal mode of address had not gone unnoticed by Frederica. She nodded. "Indeed, your ladyship. I shall manage very well. You have been kindness itself, but now you must see to your guest. I shall take my leave of you both. Good afternoon, your ladyship, your lordship." She curtseyed to each of them in turn and walked briskly away.

For some reason, the day seemed gloomier than it had, the countryside less beautiful, but the brilliant smile the Viscountess bestowed on her just before she left remained vivid all the way home.

CHAPTER 6

LORD PEREGRINE FELL into step beside Joanna, tugging the rein until the thoroughbred followed dutifully behind him. " 'Tis very selfish of you, keeping a pretty young thing like Miss Bertram to yourself, Joanna."

"Have you taken leave of your senses?"

"Don't deny it. I saw you." He tapped a finger against his nose and smiled. "You were holding hands."

"Don't talk gammon. I had upset Miss Bertram and was trying to restore her equilibrium. She is to marry Chaloner Dunster."

He laughed. "Trying to restore her equilibrium, eh? I must remember that turn of phrase."

She held her tongue. If Perry was determined to misunderstand her, it was best to let the matter drop.

"Has this Dunster fellow proposed to Miss Bertram yet?"

"No. But he will. 'Tis only a matter of time."

Perry shrugged his broad shoulders. "Since when has the fact a pretty woman is married deterred you, or me, come to that?"

Joanna grabbed his arm and dragged him to a halt.

"Mind my sleeve!" Indignantly he smoothed the marks she had left on the green cloth.

"Let me make something clear," she hissed. "While you are my guest at Thornbury Park, you will be on your best behaviour at all times. These people are my family and friends, and they matter to me. They are simple country folk, not world-weary libertines."

Lord Peregrine began to object at this description of himself but her raised finger stopped him.

"There will be no seducing of ladies, married or unmarried—no, not even the servants—no baiting of gentlemen until they are enraged into asking you to give them satisfaction. You will not humiliate or hurt anyone. You are my guest, and you will behave like one."

He pouted. "Am I to have no amusement at all?"

"This is not a joke, Perry." She dropped her voice to its lowest register. "If you do not agree to my conditions, then you had better turn round right now and ride back to London." She waited for the threat to sink in.

"As you wish."

They walked on a few paces in silence.

" 'Pon my soul, Joanna. I had forgotten how fierce you get when someone crosses you." He gave a mock shudder. "Thought it was to be pistols at dawn between us for a moment."

"I would win."

"Undoubtedly. Which is why I would never challenge you."

"I am glad we are clear on that point."

"We are indeed."

Thornbury Park was now visible up ahead. And Perry gazed at it and gave an appreciative whistle. "That is your brother's residence?"

She nodded.

"He has done well for himself."

"Edmund bought it for a song. He has always been more canny about money matters than I." She glanced at the horse trailing along behind her companion. "Which reminds me, did your father cough up the blunt?"

Lord Peregrine gave her a rueful glance. "Unfortunately not. My tiresome Papa has decided that I should take responsibility for my finances. He sent me packing without so much as a guinea."

"But surely, Lightning . . ."

"Oh, I won him in a bet." He turned and stroked the horse's nose. "Didn't I, old fellow?"

She stared at him. "What if you had lost?"

He plucked a greenfly from his waistcoat, careful not to leave a stain. "It was a sure thing."

Given her recent risk-taking activities on the Exchange, she felt unable to rebuke him for his giddiness, so she restricted herself to, "Same old Perry."

He laughed.

"So you have decided to throw yourself on my brother's mercy rather than starve?"

He gave her a wounded look. "I promised to entertain you, did I not?"

"You did indeed."

For the past few minutes, they had been walking up the drive to Thornbury Park. Now, a footman came hurrying out to greet them.

"Will you please inform my brother we have an unexpected guest, Walter?" called Joanna. "And after that, take care of Lord Peregrine's horse."

"Very good, your ladyship." The footman darted back inside.

She glanced at Lightning, who nickered and shook his mane at her. "Where are your trunks, Perry?"

"My valet is bringing them down tomorrow. I trust your brother can lend me a nightshirt in the meantime?"

"I daresay."

They closed the remaining few yards to the front door.

Walter reappeared. "Mr. and Mrs. Lynton, and Mr. Dunster, are awaiting you and your guest in the drawing room, your ladyship." He relieved Perry of his mount and led the magnificent beast round to the stables.

Joanna stepped into the hall, removing her bonnet and gloves as she did so. She handed them to the waiting Dorothea, whose dark brows drew together at the sight of Perry. Edmund's butler relieved his lordship of his top hat and gloves. Then they made their way down the passage to the drawing room.

Edmund rose to his feet as they entered, his gaze travelling to the man following Joanna. "So we are to have a guest, Joanna?"

Disquiet lurked behind his smile, though only those who knew him well would realise it. She threw him a reassuring glance. He should not regret opening his house to her, on that she was determined.

"Lord Peregrine is an old friend, Edmund. I invited him down while I was in London." Swiftly she made the introductions.

Perry's "I apologise if my unexpected arrival has put you to any inconvenience," instantly disarmed any objection they might have had. He went on to amuse Caroline with tales about Almack's and ask Edmund for advice about managing an estate as large as Thornbury Park. ("For I shall one day inherit Painswick House, and will need all the help I can get.") As for Chaloner, Perry mentioned that he had met Miss Bertram and how her appearance and manners were admirable and just as they ought to be. (All this based on a single fleeting meeting, thought Joanna wryly.) To cap it all, he drank the cup of tea Caroline handed him with every appearance of enjoyment—which since he loathed the stuff was remarkable. Joanna was torn between amusement and admiration at this display.

By the end of an hour, the matter was settled to everyone's satisfaction. Of course Lord Peregrine must stay for a while. He would be much needed company for Joanna, who had been exhibiting signs of boredom with country pursuits in recent days. Edmund laughingly overruled her protestations to the contrary, and she had to concede that she had indeed been feeling a little restless. A nightshirt was found. And servants were dispatched to make a bedchamber ready.

DOROTHEA WAS WAITING for Joanna in her chamber, her expression stormy. "What's *he* doing here?"

"I'm afraid I invited him," she admitted. "While we were staying at The George. I ran into him at Rotten Row."

A snort greeted that remark but Joanna ignored it. She divested herself of her half boots then straightened and turned her back so that her abigail could unbutton her cambric walking dress.

"It's partly your fault, you know." She turned an accusing eye in Dorothea's direction. "You told me I would be bored in the country." She stepped out of her dress. "And even you must admit, Perry is damned entertaining."

"As though you ever take notice of a thing I say," muttered Dorothea, shaking out the dress before folding it neatly, then fetching a satin evening dress from the wardrobe.

"I know. And I am sorry now." She threw her abigail a pleading glance. "But he has promised me he will behave."

"And you believe him?" Dorothea tutted.

"Perry is my friend."

"He *was* your friend, your ladyship. But you are not the person you used to be."

Joanna allowed herself to be buttoned into her dress and pulled on her matching gloves. "In any event, I have resolved to keep a close eye on him. And I have warned him most particularly to leave Frederica alone."

She bent to put on her shoes, and when she straightened found Dorothea's stern gaze fixed on her.

"Tell me you have not developed a *tendre* for her," said Dorothea.

"For who?"

"Miss Bertram, of course. I notice you are now on first name terms with the young woman."

Joanna sighed. "You too?"

"Do I need to remind you, your ladyship, of your promise not to set the cat among the pigeons in your brother's back yard? Miss Bertram is to marry Mr. Dunster. Everyone at Thornbury knows it."

"You go too far, Dorothea! Nothing of significance has happened between Fred . . . Miss Bertram and me, nor will it. I have too much respect for her, and for Edmund. But Perry showed a marked interest in her—he met her while I was escorting her back to Chawleigh House—so I must perforce warn him off." Her abigail look unconvinced. "He has agreed to behave himself while he is here," she continued, nettled. "And that's an end to it."

Dorothea sniffed. "I'm sure I beg pardon I ever doubted you, your ladyship. If you know what you are about, then I will say no more about it." She fetched her sewing box, sat down, and busied herself with her mending.

Joanna checked her appearance in the mirror and prepared to go down to dinner. For all her abigail's faith in her, did she *really* know what she was about? Sometimes she wasn't so sure.

THE NEXT MORNING found Joanna and Perry out riding. Her mount was tiring rapidly; even so, he didn't baulk at the hedge and cleared it with inches to spare.

"Whoa, Chestnut." She patted the labouring horse on the neck and reined him to a halt. "There now. Easy. You have had enough, I think." She dismounted and took off her gloves, then grabbed a handful of grass and rubbed some of the sweat from his neck and flanks. He was trembling all over. "What a brave heart you have," she murmured. "No wonder you are Edmund's favourite hunter."

Up ahead, Perry had turned back. When he was still some distance from her he shouted, "Do you concede?"

"I do. You have won your bet," she called.

The race had been uneven from the start, Edmund's hunter against Lord Peregrine's thoroughbred. Joanna had accepted more because she wanted to blow the cobwebs away than to win the wager, such as it was.

Perry halted beside her and dismounted. "I would have not won so easily in the old days."

"Indeed not. Conqueror would have been more than a match for Lightning." She threw away the grass and picked the residue of stalks and seeds off her palms before wiping them on her breeches. A green stain resulted. Dorothea would not be pleased.

"Conqueror was that fierce black beast who tried to bite me, was he not? What happened to him?"

"Lord knows. I had to sell him to pay my debts. Put out to stud somewhere, I daresay." Chestnut nudged her shoulder, and she laughed and stroked his nose. "No more brushing. My arm is tired."

She led him back the way they had come, and Perry fell in step beside her. The two horses eyed one another warily.

"My winnings?" reminded Perry.

"Forgive me." She pulled out a guinea and tossed it to him. He caught it and regarded it ruefully before pocketing it.

"In the old days, our bet would have been more substantial. This will buy Lightning a carrot or two at best."

"Those days are gone, Perry. I have turned over a new leaf. Why, just the other day, I helped my brother with the haymaking."

His eyebrows shot up. "I hope you will not expect me to do the same."

She snorted with amusement. "No. But you will not be bored. There is a ball at the assembly rooms on Friday night. That should be more to your taste."

"Ah, dancing. More to my taste indeed."

They walked on, the silence broken only by the thudding of hooves, creaking of leather, and panting of the horses. Chestnut soon recovered his wind, she was pleased to see.

Perry laughed suddenly. "Remember that cricket ball of yours? Cost me four hundred guineas, if I remember. Now *that* was a bet."

She smiled, remembering. He had not believed her claim that she could make a letter travel fifty miles in an hour. She had enclosed the letter in a hollow cricket ball and paid twenty skilled cricketers to stand in a carefully measured circle, throwing the ball to one another as fast as they could. They had more than managed the distance in the time allotted.

"It was a love letter, was it not?"

"To Florentia, my first real passion."

"Ah yes, the courtesan. Was she not fifteen years older than you?"

They stopped at a brook and allowed the horses to drink.

"Indeed," said Joanna. "Florentia taught me much about the ways of love, and for that I shall always be grateful. She also threw me over the week after the cricket ball bet. Something about my ogling the ladies in Rotten Row, if I recall." She pretended to be aggrieved, and Perry guffawed as she had intended.

"You always had a roving eye," he said. "Courtesans, actresses. The more colourful the better." He pursed his lips. "Strange. I would not have thought a country mouse like Miss Bertram would attract your attention."

She threw him an exasperated glance. "You are barking up the wrong tree, Perry. And what's worse, you are in danger of becoming a bore."

"A bore?" He pressed a hand to his heart as if wounded. "You have cut me to the quick."

"Humbug!" Joanna judged Chestnut fit to be ridden once more. "Shall we ride? I am hungry, and"—she pulled out her pocket watch and checked it— "'tis nearly time for lunch." She mounted up, and waited for Perry to do the same.

"Good." He put a booted foot in the stirrup and heaved himself into the saddle. "After last night's excellent dinner, I am eager to see what your brother's cook has prepared."

CHAPTER 7

IT WAS THE night of the ball. All day, Amelia had been driving everyone at Chawleigh to distraction with her dithering about what she should wear. She had changed her dress twice and her hairstyle three times, quite wearing out the maid in the process. Frederica had no such difficulties—only one of her evening dresses, the cream satin, would suit a ball, and she would wear her hair as she always did.

Amelia was also full of speculation about who would be there. "For if I have to dance with Mr. Smith *again* I shall surely die."

Eventually, Frederica shook her head at such histrionics and left her sister to her own devices.

When they arrived, the assembly rooms were already quite full, and while their mother went to greet her friends, and Amelia headed for the soldiers congregating at the far end near the punchbowl, Frederica scanned the milling faces. There was no sign of anyone from Thornbury Park, and she was unsure whether to be relieved or annoyed. Not dancing with Chaloner would be no loss—he seemed the type to step on her toes—but she had been looking forward to gauging the reaction to the notorious Viscountess, and, if she were honest, to renewing her acquaintance with the woman herself. She had been unable to banish their last encounter from her thoughts.

Her sister darted past, pursued by poor Herbert Smith. When next she spied them, Amelia was dancing the Boulanger with a dashing Lieutenant while Mr. Smith looked as though someone had killed his favourite dog.

"Not dancing, Miss Bertram?"

She turned to find old Squire Nicholls regarding her kindly. "Mr. Dunster claimed this first dance from me but has not yet arrived."

"A late entrance is all the rage, I believe."

As if in response to his remark, a commotion by the door drew their attention. The throng parted to allow through a party of well dressed ladies and gentlemen. Edmund and Caroline Lynton were in the lead, greeting acquaintances with broad smiles and kind words. Following behind them came a rather sulky-looking Chaloner Dunster. And bringing up the rear was a handsome couple whose height, clothes, carriage, and demeanour were attracting glances and murmurs of admiration, envy, and not a little outrage.

Frederica stared along with the rest. Joanna was wearing a crimson-velvet ball dress, with a frill *à la Parisienne*, and white kid gloves and shoes. Pearls studded her raven-black hair. She looked magnificent.

"Who is that?" asked the Squire.

She came to herself with a start. "Viscountess Norland and Lord Peregrine, eldest son of the Earl of Painswick."

"You are very well informed, Miss Bertram."

She blushed then wondered why she had. "To be sure. For the Lyntons are our closest neighbours."

Chaloner spotted her and made his way towards her. She summoned up a welcoming smile.

"Miss Bertram."

"Mr. Dunster."

"I apologise for missing the first dance. Edmund insisted we wait for the entire party. Who would have believed a neckcloth could take so much tying?" The glance he threw Lord Peregrine was filled with irritation.

Meanwhile, the orchestra had struck up a cotillion, and couples were taking their places in a square. Lord Peregrine had lost no time in finding himself a pretty young partner, she saw. The girl's eyes were bright with excitement, her colour so high Frederica feared she might faint.

Chaloner assumed a gallant expression that unfortunately put her in mind of a cow. "May I have this dance?"

"With pleasure," she lied, allowing him to lead her out onto the floor.

By the time the dance had run its course, her toes were smarting and her temper was on edge. Her shame-faced partner helped her limp to a seat while he went in search of refreshment.

"There goes a medical curiosity. For surely Mr. Dunster has two left feet."

The familiar voice made her twist round in her seat. Joanna was standing behind her, eyes twinkling. Frederica gave her a quelling look, which caused Joanna's smile to broaden.

"But I'm sure you would say," continued the irrepressible Viscountess, "that Mr. Dunster has the *intention* to dance well, he merely lacks the means."

"I would do no such thing," hissed Frederica. "Please, your ladyship. He will be back any moment."

"Tut, Frederica. Back to 'your ladyship,' I see. And what are Mr. Dunster's feelings to me, pray? He has no concern for mine." But she changed the topic. "Now *there* is a much better dancer."

Frederica followed Joanna's gaze to where Lord Peregrine was dancing the Sir Roger de Coverley with yet another pretty young woman. A young lieutenant glared daggers at him.

"If looks could kill," murmured Joanna.

"Indeed. Is that wise of him?"

"Perry is never wise. There is no amusement in it."

At that moment, Chaloner pushed his way between the bystanders and came towards them, a glass in each hand. He gave Joanna a cold glance and handed Frederica a glass, which proved to contain orgeat. She would have preferred punch, but tried to look as though she was enjoying the excessively sweet almond-flavoured lemonade—perhaps with not much success, for Joanna laughed under her breath and moved away.

When later Frederica saw the Viscountess, she was dancing a waltz with Lord Peregrine, every eye in the place fixed on them. The waltz was still considered scandalous by many due to the close embrace it necessitated, but apparently Lord Peregrine had particularly requested it. She frowned and looked away, annoyed with Joanna yet not sure why. Later, when his lordship was dancing a reel with Amelia—their third dance in a row together—there was no sign of the Viscountess, and enquiries revealed she had grown bored and left early.

Disappointed, Frederica went to join her mother, who was watching Amelia and Perry with unabashed delight.

"Their third dance! What a catch he would be for your sister, Frederica."

"I do not think it either likely or wise, Mama."

"Oh pooh! What do you know about it, pray?"

Chaloner came up beside her. "May I have the next dance, Miss Bertram?"

"You may," she said glumly, and, when the orchestra struck up a quadrille, a dance that was still so new she was doubtful she would remember the steps and certain he would not, she wished the evening well and truly over.

A SURPRISE VISIT the next day from Frederica's oldest brother Charles, his wife Louisa, and their two small children, kept her from her appointment with Chaloner. She did not regret it. She feared from his behaviour towards her at the ball that their next meeting would be significant. And so it proved. For when she saw him three days later, Viscountess Norland was out with Lord Peregrine, and without her presence to daunt him and with his sister's prompting and support, Chaloner formally asked Frederica to be his wife.

It could have been worse, she supposed. At least there had been no pretence of ardour on his part when he raised her hand to his lips. She had pictured herself accepting his proposal, but now the moment had arrived, indecision paralysed her. If the mere thought of it made her heart sink, what kind of a marriage lay in prospect? One which would see her comfortably provided for, and which her family would seize on with relief, certainly. But was that enough? Chaloner was a good man, a gentle if rather dull man, she reminded herself. Such a match was unlikely to come her way again. Refuse it and she was likely condemning herself to old maidhood. But still she could not decide.

Frederica stuttered her thanks to Chaloner for the great honour he had done her, begged for time to consider his proposal, and promised a reply when next they met. Then, under the Dunster siblings' equally disappointed gazes, she made good her escape.

As she climbed the stairs up to the schoolroom in search of her sister, raised voices, a man's and a woman's, met her.

"This is insupportable!"

"You are making a mountain out of a molehill, Joanna. It is not as if I am pursuing her sister."

Frederica turned the corner into the passageway and halted. Viscountess Norland and Lord Peregrine were standing nose to nose outside the schoolroom door. The Viscountess's cheeks were flushed with fury. His lordship was affecting amused boredom, but Frederica thought she detected irritation in his gaze.

They broke off their conversation at her appearance. Joanna smoothed her expression into a bland mask while he donned polished charm.

"Miss Bertram." Lord Peregrine bowed. "Have you come in search of your sister?"

She curtsied. "Yes, your lordship, your ladyship."

Joanna gestured. "She is in the schoolroom." Her tone was brusque, but Frederica sensed that she was not the target and took no offence.

"Thank you." As nonchalantly as she could manage, she moved past them, knocked on the door, and, at her sister's muffled "Enter," turned the handle and pushed it open.

A scuffling noise and an exclamation made her turn, in time to see Joanna hurrying Lord Peregrine away, her iron grip on his sleeve prompting outraged protests. She shook her head in wonder and continued into the schoolroom.

Amelia was trying to settle a squabble—the three Lynton children had very decided ideas about which toys they should play with. She looked up and gave Frederica a harassed glance. "Is it time to depart?"

"Yes. We must leave at once."

The announcement prompted much whining and clinging as the children realised they were to lose their Aunt Amelia, but a promise that she would soon come again settled them. Amelia put on her bonnet and gloves, and told them to play quietly, then went next door to fetch the children's governess, Miss Lang.

With difficulty, Frederica held her tongue all the way down the stairs and out of Thornbury Park's front door. Halfway down the gravelled drive though, she felt able to speak.

"What in the world is going on, Amelia? Viscountess Norland and Lord Peregrine were arguing outside your door."

Amelia rolled her eyes. "Oh Lord. It was too tiresome for words, Frederica. She marched right in without so much as a by your leave, told his lordship he had no right to be there, and practically dragged him outside. We were having such a pleasant time too. The children were distraught."

Frederica blinked and missed a step. "Lord Peregrine was with you? Unchaperoned?"

"As if any of that matters," said Amelia crossly. "He only came to assist me with the children, and the governess was next door all the time."

"That is not the point."

Her sister waved a dismissive hand. "The Viscountess is merely jealous, for she sees that I might get him instead of her."

"Get him? Amelia, the Viscountess is already married."

"That doesn't signify." Amelia gave a dreamy sigh. "He *is* handsome, is he not? Much better looking than Mr. Herbert, and much more amusing besides. And such a good dancer. Did I tell you he danced three times with me at the ball? I did? And Lord Peregrine danced only *once* with poor Georgette Fontley. She was so annoyed she could cry."

Frederica sighed.

"Did you see his clothes? His neckcloth is the latest style." Amelia twirled her reticule. "He was telling me all about Painswick House. He will inherit it when his father dies, you know."

"This will not do, Amelia. He belongs to the fast set. Papa will be furious."

"Fiddlesticks. He was the perfect gentleman, and so good with the children." She glanced at Frederica. "Besides, who are you to begrudge me his company? You have Chaloner." She blinked as though remembering something. "Has he offered for you?" Frederica nodded, and her sister clapped her hands and skipped a few steps. "Mama will be pleased. You accepted him, I take it?"

"Not yet."

A shocked gasp met that admission. "Are you mad? After all your efforts to bring him to this point? Whatever possessed you, Frederica? No wonder you are so sour about me and Lord Peregrine."

"The one has nothing to do with the other."

Her sister shot her an arch glance. "Indeed."

They walked on, Amelia babbling about everything and nothing, Frederica's thoughts whirling.

"Lord Peregrine says the Viscountess is not as amusing as she once was."

The mention of Joanna caught Frederica's attention,   and she looked up. "I beg your pardon?"

"She used to make outrageous bets with him. There was something about a letter inside a cricket ball, I believe."

"A cricket ball?" Frederica gave her sister a bewildered glance.

"And climbing up a steep tower to hang a pair of lady's drawers from a flagpole."

Frederica was shocked. She had known her sister was lax in her attitudes, but to talk of undergarments with a man while unchaperoned . . . "Really, Amelia!"

"And once," continued her sister, unperturbed, "she recreated the Duke of Queensberry's Race Against Time, only she drove the carriage herself."

Intrigued by Amelia's chattering in spite of herself, Frederica tried to remember the details. Was that not the wager that a four-wheeled carriage drawn by four horses could travel nineteen miles in an hour? Old Q, as he was known, had stripped away the frame, removed the seat, and used silk traces and silk-and-whalebone harnesses. With nothing to sit on or cling to, and the roads so poor, it was immensely dangerous. The Duke's groom had managed the feat though. And so, apparently, had Joanna.

"She could have been killed," said Frederica, appalled.

But Amelia's attention had already moved on.

Frederica returned to her own concerns, her thoughts so fragmented they were making her dizzy. One minute she was picturing herself as Mrs. Chaloner Dunster, Mistress of Symond Hall, the next she was wondering what Lord Peregrine could possible want with her silly sister. And as for that snatch of conversation she had overheard: "It is not as if I am pursuing her sister." Had Joanna and Lord Peregrine been talking about her?

By the time they reached Chawleigh House Frederica had a headache, and when Amelia went skipping indoors, shouting out to anyone within earshot, "Mama, Chaloner has proposed to Frederica but she has not accepted him," she knew the ordeal had just begun.

MRS. BERTRAM PRESSED a hand to her breast. Her face was pale, and she looked as though she were about to faint. "What is this about Mr. Dunster proposing and you not accepting him, Frederica?"

"*Yet.*" Frederica shot her sister an annoyed glance. "I have not accepted him yet, Mama."

"Thank heavens." Her mother collapsed back into her chair. "For a moment . . . Well, no matter. You will accept his proposal tomorrow, and that will be the end of it."

"But I am by no means certain I will accept him."

Mrs. Bertram's hand flew to her mouth. "Why, whatever can you mean?"

Mr. Bertram looked up from his newspaper in surprise.

"Yes, Frederica," added Amelia. "How can you be so selfish? For you must know that if you do not marry it will blight my prospects considerably."

"Amelia!" Mr. Bertram frowned her to silence and turned a grave gaze on Frederica. "What is it that disturbs you about the match, my dear?"

"Oh do not pander to her," said his wife, her tone one of vexation. "She is being foolish. Tell her to accept his offer at once."

"I will do no such thing, Mrs. Bertram. Frederica's happiness is important to me. And I venture to say that, out of all this family, she is the one person who is never foolish."

Both Amelia and her mother blinked at this bald statement.

"Your thoughts on the matter, Frederica," persisted her father.

She reddened and fiddled with her gloves. "I am not sure I know them myself, Papa."

"You do not love Mr. Dunster, I take it?"

"No, Papa."

"Good heavens, is that all?" said her mother. "I did not love Mr. Bertram when I married him but I knew my duty."

"Indeed," murmured Mr. Bertram. "And now look where we are." He addressed Frederica once more. "But he is kind to you, and fond of you, is he not?"

"Yes, Papa."

"And you would be mistress of Symond Hall," added Amelia. "Think of that!"

"She would indeed," said Mr. Bertram. "But you do not think all this will be enough to make you happy, Frederica?"

"I fear not."

Mrs. Bertram's exclamation drew a stern glance from her husband, and she subsided.

"Do you know what *would* make you happy?"

"No, Papa," said Frederica miserably. "I beg your pardon."

"Well, well. No need to apologise, my dear. You take after me, I fear. A face and figure others deem pleasing, good clothes, and a comfortable life are enough for your brothers and sister, but your intelligence is too keen for such things alone to make you truly happy."

"Oh, pshaw!" said her mother. "Do not go putting such ideas into her head, Mr. Bertram. She will come to love Mr. Dunster, and if she does not, well in time she will have her own children to dote on and a country house to run. What more could she want?"

"What more indeed?"

His gaze locked with Frederica's, and she knew that her father understood her. She also realised what it was she wanted: an affectionate companion of the heart and the mind; someone to share her most intimate thoughts with, to laugh with her and maybe even at her, if it was kindly meant, and to agree with her opinions or challenge them if she was in error. Someone who was always lively, honest, and interesting. And most of all someone who would understand her and make her feel cherished. That someone was not Chaloner Dunster. But knowing that did not help her decision one jot.

"And if she refuses Mr. Dunster, what is to become of her?" continued Mrs. Bertram. "Is she to be a spinster in a mobcap? For such a fortunate match will not come her way again, you can be sure."

"If wearing such a cap would make our daughter happy, then that is what I would encourage her to do. But alas, I fear it would not."

"Oh! It is all that detestable woman's fault! I told you not to let our daughters keep company with her, Mr. Bertram, but you would overrule me, and this is the result."

"I take it you are referring to Viscountess Norland? And how, precisely, is this her fault?"

"She has set a bad example with her own marriage. And now Frederica looks set to follow her."

"I hardly think the circumstances are the same, Mrs. Bertram. But in any case, that is beside the point." He folded his paper, rose, and crossed to stand beside Frederica. "You must make this decision for yourself, my dear." He rested his hand on her shoulder. "For you alone will bear the consequences."

She sighed. "I know, Papa."

"But whatever you decide, whether it is to marry Mr. Dunster or stay with us, or to become a governess of someone else's shrieking brats, or a companion to a cantankerous old widow, I will endorse your choice as long as it makes you happy."

"She cannot stay here with us," protested Mrs. Bertram. "You know how much it costs to house our daughters. Why, only the other day you were recommending economies—"

Frederica's father turned and stopped his wife with a raised hand. "Ay, to *you*, Madam. Frederica has ever been economical. But that is not the issue here. And I have made my position clear." Regarding Frederica once more, he said, "Decide for yourself, my dear, but think carefully and do not take too long."

FREDERICA HAD JUST finished her breakfast and sat down to reread *Pride and Prejudice*, hoping it would calm her perturbation to lose herself in fiction, when she heard a commotion at the front door. She left the drawing room and headed along the passage towards the hall.

Mr. Bertram had that morning ridden over to see his steward, so in his absence, their mother was greeting the guest. She simpered at someone Frederica could not yet see, asking him "to what did they owe the honour?" The butler relieved their visitor of his hat, cane, and gloves, then her mother stepped aside and revealed his identity. Lord Peregrine.

Frederica's pulse raced as she searched for Viscountess Norland, who must surely have accompanied his lordship. He was alone.

Disappointed and puzzled, she stepped forward, just as he answered, "I have come to pay my respects to your daughter, Madam."

"To Frederica?"

"Your *other* daughter." His gaze fell on Frederica, and he bowed and said gallantly, "Not that both aren't as pretty as a picture. But your eldest daughter is spoken for, is she not?"

Mrs. Bertram smiled. "Indeed we believe so."

Since Frederica had still not been able to make up her mind, and had spent the night tossing and turning and when she did sleep, having the most dreadful nightmares, she kept quiet.

Her curtsey in response to his lordship's bow attracted her mother's attention at last. "Don't just stand there, Frederica. Go and fetch Amelia. We must not keep his lordship waiting. This way, Lord Peregrine."

With a last curious glance, Frederica made her way upstairs to the bedchamber she shared with her sister. On learning who her visitor was, Amelia became all of a fluster. She wanted to change into a less shabby and more flattering dress, or if not that, into different shoes at least. And was her hair not looking most ugly today? The maid had done a slapdash job; perhaps she should call her to redress it—

"Good lord," said Frederica, her patience at an end. "Every moment you delay leaves him to Mama's tender mercies, and you know how mortifying she can be. At this very moment, she is probably entertaining Lord Peregrine with stories of your most embarrassing exploits, from babyhood to the present day. If not, then she is cataloguing your accomplishments, and as always excusing your singing because you look so charming while doing it even if you cannot hold a tune, and—"

But Amelia was already out of the bedchamber and halfway down the stairs. Frederica rolled her eyes and followed at a more sedate pace, still puzzling on the whereabouts of the missing Viscountess, who surely would not have allowed her friend to come here on his own.

She took her seat next to her sister and regarded Lord Peregrine closely. Handsome he had been, she allowed, though his looks were fading fast, and even his *á la mode* clothes and hairstyle couldn't disguise the fact. He must be at least fifteen years older than Amelia, and if he was anything like Joanna had travelled extensively. She could not imagine what such a man could possibly see in her giddy young sister.

"And you, Miss Bertram?" With a start, she became aware that his keen gaze was fixed on her. "Are you well? You look tired, if you will forgive the observation. Unlike your sister who is positively vibrant this morning."

Amelia beamed at the remark.

"I am well enough," said Frederica, nettled in spite of herself and aware of the amused glint in his eyes. Now was her chance. "I am surprised the Viscountess did not accompany you."

His smile widened. "It is so like you to concern yourself with her affairs, Miss Bertram. She was called away on business." He turned to her mother and explained, "A house in the neighbourhood has taken her fancy, and she has gone to discuss terms with the house agent."

The smile vanished from Mrs. Bertram's face. "Viscountess Norland is thinking of residing in Kent permanently?" Her dismay was obvious, and Frederica flushed at such rudeness.

"Astonishing, is it not?" continued Lord Peregrine unperturbed. "It could simply be that she wishes to remain near her brother, to be sure, but I doubt that. There must be something else in the county that attracts her."

His eyes locked with Frederica's as he spoke, and he arched an eyebrow. She dropped her gaze, thoughts whirling. To what was he referring?

"But I fear we are boring Miss Amelia. Do you ride, my dear?"

"Not as often as I would like," came her sister's reply. "For Papa is always taking the horse for his own use and never thinks of my needs."

Frederica kept her jaw from dropping with some difficulty. She tried to catch her sister's eye, but Amelia was deliberately ignoring her.

"I rode over on my latest acquisition," said Lord Peregrine. "Lightning's a thoroughbred. Too high-spirited a mount for a lady in normal circumstances. But if I were to lead him while the lady in question rode him, I daresay he would be docile enough. What do you say, Miss Amelia?" He gave her a winning smile. "Care to try him?"

Amelia clapped her hands in delight. "May I, Mama?"

Frederica leaned forward and murmured to her mother, "Is this not very forward for so early an acquaintance?"

But Mrs. Bertram waved her away. "Where is the harm?" She raised her voice. "Of course you may, Amelia. Especially since his lordship assures me it is perfectly safe. Is that not so, your lordship?"

"Indeed it is, dear lady." He beamed at her and rose. "No time like the present, eh?"

They decamped outside to where Lightning had been tethered and was contentedly cropping the grass. Amelia was immediately lovesick for the bay horse, and could not stop cooing and petting him. For his part, Lightning became skittish and refused to be touched, until Lord Peregrine rubbed him on the nose and muttered something in his ear. After that, he seemed resigned to his fate.

Amelia instructed a servant to fetch her sidesaddle, and Lord Peregrine obligingly replaced his saddle with hers. Then he lifted her up, waited for her to make herself comfortable, and started leading Lightning up and down in front of the house.

It was impossible to overhear the low conversation between the beautiful rider and her aristocratic groom, but whatever it concerned seemed to elicit laughter from him and many brilliant glances from her. Though her mother was looking on with delight, Frederica became more and more concerned. She could have sworn that his lordship rested his hand on her sister's knee at one point, and worse still that Amelia did not object. But when he turned the horse round and led it back towards Frederica and her mother, there was no sign of the errant hand.

She wished her father were here, or Joanna come to that. They would know how to deal with the predatory Lord, she was sure, whereas her mother patently did not. Indeed, so taken was she with the magnificence of Amelia's catch, she was practically throwing her youngest daughter at him.

CHAPTER 8

IT WAS WITH a sense of satisfaction that Viscountess Norland turned her brother's gig towards Thornbury Park. Mr. Barton had driven a hard bargain, but she had driven a harder one. Murviton was just the thing—the house was a good deal smaller than Thornbury, to be sure, and the grounds a tenth the size, but though the furnishings were sadly faded, the house itself was in excellent repair, and its rent was well within her financial compass. Besides, she had imposed on her brother long enough.

She imagined herself taking the air in Murviton's rose garden with a certain young woman with fine green eyes, then chided herself for her foolishness. Frederica would probably marry Mr. Dunster, and he would spirit her off to Norfolk, and that would be an end to it.

"Do you think you will like your new home, Dorothea?"

"It's certainly an improvement on that hovel in Paris, your ladyship," said the abigail, who was sitting beside her.

"Hovel? I emptied my purse paying for that establishment."

"Two paltry rooms, and cockroaches everywhere." Dorothea sniffed. "I grew used to the sound of crunching underfoot."

Joanna stifled a grin. "There should be few cockroaches at Murviton."

"So I should hope." The gig travelled on a little before Dorothea pursed her lips and said, "But I cannot run such a large establishment alone, your ladyship."

"No indeed. You shall hire as many servants as you see fit. Within reason, of course. My finances may presently be flush, thanks to the Iron Duke, but let us not go overboard."

She pushed back her bonnet to allow the summer breeze to cool her face, and found herself grinning. "My own country house. What a novelty!"

"Rented," reminded Dorothea.

"Ay. But it's a start."

"You do not think you will be bored to tears, remaining in one place?"

Joanna raised an eyebrow. "We shall still go visiting."

"To Chawleigh?" Dorothea's gaze was sly.

Joanna snorted. "You know me too well. But I fear Miss Bertram will be lost to the clutches of Mr. Dunster soon. I was thinking more of Edmund. It has been wonderful being on terms with him again. I had forgotten the pleasures of family."

"And the horrors of offspring."

"His children *are* rather hard on both the ears and the clothes," agreed Joanna, thinking of an incident involving young George Lynton, a glass of lemonade, and her new kid half boots. "But I plan to stay out of their way until they attain maturity."

"What about Lord Peregrine, your ladyship?"

"What about him?"

"Will he be welcome at Murviton?"

"I see no reason why not. But he will probably wish to give me a wide berth. For he says I have become boring company these days."

"And about time too."

"You were meant to say I am not boring."

Her abigail's eyes gleamed. "I know."

The Viscountess turned the gig into the gravelled drive and started the approach to Thornbury Park. "Tut! Why I put up with your impertinence I do not know."

"Because I put up with your bad temper?"

"Very likely." Edmund's footman had come out to greet them. She brought the horse to a stop. "Thank you, Walter." She handed him the reins, and stepped down.

"Er herm, your ladyship."

His cheeks had reddened, and she paused, intrigued. "Yes?"

"Miss Bertram arrived but a moment ago, dishevelled and winded from running."

Joanna frowned. For Frederica to run all the way from Chawleigh, something must be wrong.

"She is in the drawing room with Mr. Lynton," continued the footman. "But she came seeking you. I thought you would wish to know."

"Thank you, Walter. That was kindly done. I will go there directly."

She didn't stop to discard her hat and gloves, but headed straight along the passage towards the drawing room.

"You must be mistaken, Miss Bertram." The door muffled Edmund's voice. "No friend of my sister's would do such a thing."

"No one would more gladly be mistaken than I. But Amelia is missing."

Without ceremony, Joanna pushed open the door. Two heads, one as dark as her own, one fair, turned to face her.

Frederica gave a glad cry, "Joanna!" and ran towards her, gloved hands reaching. "Is Lord Peregrine with you? Oh please say he is."

"Perry? Why no. I left him in Edmund's care." The hope in Frederica's eyes died, and Joanna took her hands and pressed them. She turned to regard her brother. "You said you would show him round the estate, Edmund."

"He left soon after you. Pressing business of some kind." He shrugged. "I could not stop him, sister. But surely, Miss Bertram must be mistaken. Your friend would not do such a thing."

She kept her disquiet to herself. "Perry has not returned from his pressing business yet?"

"No."

Joanna turned back to Frederica. "What exactly is the matter? Tell me, my dear." She led the young woman back to her seat, and they both sat down.

"He came to see Amelia this morning. Lord Peregrine, I mean. He talked with Mama, and let Amelia ride Lightning. Now there is no sign of him or his horse. And Amelia is missing."

"What are you saying? Perry and Amelia?"

"I fear so," said Frederica, distressed. "Papa was visiting a friend so Mama was supposed to be chaperoning my sister. But she was convinced that Lord Peregrine was interested in making an offer and left them alone together."

"But surely, you—"

Green eyes flashed. "You must know I would never willingly leave my sister alone with that man, Joanna."

"I beg your pardon."

"The housekeeper needed to consult about something and as my mother was busy with our visitor . . ."

Joanna's mind was whirling. Eloping with a pretty young woman smitten with his charms was just the kind of thing Perry would do for a jape. And once he had had his amusement, he would toss her away like a creased neckcloth, with no thought for her ruined reputation. But to do such a thing to Amelia, when he knew how Joanna felt about her sister . . .

That thought gave her pause, and a nasty idea began to germinate. Though she had kept her lucrative speculation on the Exchange secret, her old friend now knew she had money enough to rent her own residence. What if this were merely an attempt to secure some for himself?

Movement in the doorway turned out to be Joanna's abigail, her eyes bright with curiosity.

"Dorothea," she called. "Will you see if Perry's valet is in his chamber?"

Dorothea nodded and hurried away. Moments later she was back, her face grim. "He is gone, your ladyship. And taken all his master's trunks with him."

"'S blood!" The oath slipped out before she could stop it, and she threw Frederica an apologetic glance. "I am afraid you are correct," she told her. "That rogue has almost certainly eloped with your sister." Pale cheeks went even paler, and she feared Frederica might faint. She patted her hand. "But all is not yet lost."

Joanna turned to her brother. "A fast horse if you please, Edmund, and a light carriage that will seat three—your dogcart will do." He nodded and darted out into the passage where she heard him issuing instructions. To Dorothea she said, "Fetch me the box on my bedside table. And the money bag from the bottom drawer."

Dorothea's eyes widened but she did as she was bid.

"Will you come with me, Frederica? Your sister may need you."

Frederica visibly pulled herself together. "Of course."

"But where will you go, Joanna?" Edmund had returned. "Painswick House?"

She snorted. "The last place Perry will go is to his father's residence. No, he will hide in one of his favourite haunts. I will run him to earth there."

"But what if he has gone somewhere quite different," broke in Frederica. "What if you cannot trace—?"

"He knows I will not let him take your sister without a fight. It is the one aspect of this affair that gives me hope."

Frederica stared at her. "I don't understand."

Joanna couldn't meet her gaze. "I am his target." Guilt threatened to overwhelm her. She should have known she could not leave her past behind so easily. She had brought Lord Peregrine into her brother's house, and this was the result. "Amelia is but a bargaining chip, a means of extorting money from me."

Frederica looked dazed. "But I thought he was rich!"

"Stony broke," corrected Joanna. "His father has cut him off."

Walter appeared in the doorway. "The dogcart is ready, your ladyship." He turned to address Edmund. "And Chestnut is in the traces, as requested, Mr. Lynton."

Her brother nodded. "Thank you, Walter."

Dorothea eased past the footman into the drawing room. "Here are the items you requested, your ladyship."

Joanna transferred two rolls of banknotes and several handfuls of guineas to her reticule then handed the depleted money bag back to Dorothea in exchange for the walnut-veneered box. "Come, Frederica. There is no more time to waste if we are to save your sister's reputation."

She strode along the passageway, Frederica hard on her heels, and was heading for the front door when a man's voice called, "Miss Bertram. Miss Bertram. Wait, please. No one told me you were here. Have you come to give me your answer?"

Joanna spun on her heel and saw Chaloner Dunster coming across the vestibule towards them. She glanced at Frederica, whose cheeks were now a flaming red.

"Mr. Dunster, I—" Words failed Frederica, and she threw a pleading glance at Joanna.

"I'm afraid, Mr. Dunster, that Miss Bertram and I are bent on urgent business. She must give you your reply on her return."

He looked put out. "But—"

"On her *return*," repeated Joanna, frowning.

If looks could kill she would have been lying dead on the floor, but she couldn't have cared less.

"Come, my dear. Our carriage awaits." Placing the palm of her hand in the small of Frederica's back, she guided her firmly out the front door.

JOANNA GLANCED AT her wan companion. "Are you well, Frederica?"

They had been travelling in silence for quarter of an hour, Joanna concentrating on controlling Chestnut, who had at first fought against the traces but was now resigned to pulling the dogcart.

"My sister," came the simple reply.

"Indeed. But if it is any consolation, I am convinced Lord Peregrine, for all his faults, will not harm Amelia. She is but a sprat to catch a mackerel." She chewed her lower lip. "Though it will undoubtedly distress your sister to learn it."

Anxious eyes regarded her. "What if you are wrong?"

"I am not. But if I am, and he has harmed her . . ." She patted the object on her lap.

"What is that?"

She handed the box to Frederica, who blinked at its weight and almost dropped it. Joanna flicked the reins, and Chestnut increased his pace. A soft *snick* from beside her proved to be the catch being unhooked. She watched from the corner of her eye as Frederica eased the polished case open.

Frederica's eyes widened at the sight of the two Manton duelling pistols snuggling in the velvet interior. "You mean to use these?" Her voice was a mere whisper.

"Only as a last resort."

Frederica gave the deadly weapons a last look, then closed the box and snicked the catch closed. Joanna was pleased she hadn't thrown a fit or swooned. Frederica continued to grow in her estimation.

All at once they were in a village, Chestnut's hooves and the dogcart's large wheels splashing through a stream and making a gaggle of geese honk with alarm. Startled looks from the villagers followed their progress, then they were out the other side and speeding through the Kent countryside once more.

After a few more miles, the signpost for Dover appeared up ahead. With a feeling of relief, Joanna slowed Chestnut and swung the dogcart onto the turnpike. The going should be easier from now on.

"Dover?" said Frederica. "I would have thought London the more likely destination."

"Perry will be planning to leave for the Continent as soon as he is in funds." Joanna threw her companion a rueful glance. "This will not be the first time England has grown too hot for him."

"You speak as though from personal experience."

She nodded. "I am not proud of my past, Frederica. I was very wild. But I cannot change it, for all I might wish to."

"No indeed. We can only learn to live with our pasts, no matter how disreputable."

Joanna gave her an indulgent smile. "I do not think there can be much that is disreputable in *your* past, my dear."

For a few minutes, there was silence except for the rumbling of the wheels and the clopping of Chestnut's hooves, then Frederica turned to look at her again. "Do you visit your husband and child? You never speak of them."

Of all the remarks Joanna had expected, that had not been among them. "No."

Colour flooded Frederica's cheeks. "I beg your pardon. It is painful for you, and none of my concern."

Joanna sighed. "You mistake the reason for my reticence. It is not that I find it painful so much as . . . I am ashamed."

"Of deserting them?"

"Is *that* the account they give of me? No, do not answer. I can see from your expression that it is." She smiled a little bitterly. "I can imagine only too well the lurid tales. It is of no matter. I have grown inured to what people think of me." She realised that this statement was no longer true, and said, surprised, "Though I find I do care that *you* have a good opinion of me."

Frederica looked confused.

Joanna hesitated for a long moment then took the plunge. "The bargain was always that I would leave once I had produced an heir and make no claim on Norland's estate."

"Bargain?"

"The Viscount does not much like women, Frederica." This was something of an understatement, considering the succession of young Adonises that Norland used to invite to his country estate, but she would rather not shock the sheltered young woman sitting beside her. "But he badly needed an heir and thought with my looks I would produce him a handsome one."

She smiled at Frederica's expression. "I know I am considered striking. Why should I pretend otherwise?" She found it charming that Frederica examined her gloves, cheeks pinking.

"For a considerable sum," continued Joanna, "I agreed to marry Norland and give him an heir." She suppressed a shudder. "It is fortunate that our firstborn was not a girl, or I should have had to endure more of his attentions. The day our son was born, the Viscount took him from me and gave him to a wet nurse."

"Oh, that was cruel of him indeed."

"Was it?" She shrugged. "I did not care. The boy was but a means to an end."

"That sounds so cold-blooded." Frederica looked shocked.

"It sounds so because it was so. I was young and heartless and craved travel and adventure. And I had not the means to satisfy that craving."

"Even so, the Viscount took advantage of you. You were but what age when you married?"

"Twenty."

"And he a great deal older."

"One and twenty years older to be exact." Frederica's determination to see good in her touched her. "But that is beside the point. Do not waste your sympathy on me, my dear. I got what I wanted from the bargain."

"Not your son."

"No, not him. But then, I did not want him. And by all accounts he has grown up a spoiled and objectionable youth." She glanced at Frederica. "You will think me unnatural, but it is the truth."

"How could the Viscount do such a thing?"

"Very easily, my dear. I had signed a document agreeing to give the boy up and leave immediately after the birth."

"Had he no second thoughts?"

"None. And he held me to the letter of my agreement. I was fortunate Dorothea was with me, for I could barely walk. I collected the money—Norland is a man of his word, at least—and left, never to return."

There was silence while Frederica considered what she had heard. "A considerable sum, you said?"

"Ten thousand pounds." Joanna's smile was rueful. "And within two years I had spent it all."

Frederica blinked. "*All* of it?"

"Every guinea." Chestnut was slowing, so she flicked the rein. "There. You see, Frederica? I am every bit as bad as Perry. I sold my child for money."

"The person you were *then* did," said her companion stoutly, "but I do not think the person you are *now* would do such a thing."

Joanna smiled.

"But if you spent it all . . ."

"Oh, I have recouped that sum and more and spent it many times over since," said Joanna. "Dorothea and I have often lived on stale crusts but never for long. I am nothing if not resourceful."

"So if Perry . . . Lord Peregrine demands money, you can afford to pay him?"

"I have no intention of paying him what he demands."

Frederica raised a hand to her mouth. "But my sister!"

"Be easy. I will pay him what he *needs*, for old times' sake." Joanna patted the box on her lap. "And these will back my play."

"Old times' sake?"

"He was a good friend once." She turned to look at Frederica. "I will not let any harm come to your sister. His lordship is at this very moment waiting for me to come to him, I am sure of it."

"What if you are wrong?"

"I am not. I know him."

"Not well enough to anticipate this latest exploit."

She deserved that. "Alas, I relaxed my guard. Once, I would have seen this coming. But lately . . . Well, lately I have been distracted by other matters." Such as a modest manner, a pretty face, and a fine pair of green eyes.

They were nearing a coaching inn called The Crown, and she reined in Chestnut to a trot. "So," she said quietly. "Will you trust me, Frederica? Tell me now."

For a moment there was silence, then, "I will, Joanna."

The murmured reply brought a smile to Joanna's face and a warm glow to her heart.

CHAPTER 9

"STAY HERE. I will enquire within." The Viscountess handed Frederica the reins.

"Oh! May I not—?"

But Joanna had already leaped down, refused the attentions of the ostler running towards them, and disappeared inside The Crown.

"Upon my word! She is *my* sister," grumbled Frederica, settling herself to wait as patiently as she was able.

A few minutes later the Viscountess reappeared at the inn's entrance, her expression frustrated. "No sign of them, not even for five guineas' reward."

Frederica's heart sank, but she said nothing. Joanna hopped up onto the two-wheeled carriage, took the reins from her, and set them in motion once more.

Five miles farther down the turnpike, The Bell's landlord proved just as ignorant of their quarry. Frederica was by now conjuring up scenes that would not have been out of place in a novel of the sensational sort. She became aware that pale blue eyes were regarding her keenly. A hand reached across and pressed hers.

"Do not give up hope yet. We have scarce begun, Frederica. There must be fifteen coaching inns on this route."

"What if you are wrong? What if even now he and Amelia are at Dover, taking ship for France?"

Joanna shook her head. "On what will they live? Air? No, my dear. It will not do."

The Viscountess's reasoning gave Frederica some comfort. But there was no sign of their quarry at either The Black Swan, The Bull, or The Star and Garter. A milestone announced they were halfway to Dover, and a look at Frederica's pocket watch indicated it was getting on for dinnertime when they turned into The King's Head.

The Viscountess gave the dogcart into the care of an ostler, asking him to water the flagging horse and apportioning money for a nosebag. Then she took Frederica upstairs to the dining room for a cold collation, overriding her protests with a brusque, "My dear, you must eat something for the good of your health."

Though they had both missed lunch several hours ago, anxiety had diminished Frederica's appetite, and she was able to force down only a few mouthfuls of cold pork. Joanna's appetite was heartier, and Frederica contented herself with watching her companion eat, glad that the seat was more comfortable than the dogcart's hard bench.

At length the Viscountess set aside her plate and wiped her lips on a napkin. She beckoned the waiter, gave him some coins, and requested quietly, "Would you ask the landlord if he would be so kind as to attend me?"

He nodded and departed. Joanna rose, walked to the window, and looked out. After a moment, Frederica joined her. They were regarding the activity in the yard below—a packed stage was in the process of leaving—when the sound of the door opening made them turn.

A little man with side-whiskers, his ample stomach straining a brown cloth coat at the seams, came bustling into the dining room. "And how may I help you, ladies?"

Joanna regarded him gravely. "We are in pursuit of a couple—a gentleman of five-and-thirty and a young woman of nineteen, this lady's sister." She gestured at Frederica. "We believe they travelled this road today."

"Indeed." The landlord became thoughtful.

"The gentleman is about my height, his clothes and hair tending towards the dandyish. The young woman is a little taller than my companion and fuller of figure. She is fair, very pretty, and dressed in—" She turned to Frederica and raised an eyebrow.

"A Turkey red muslin morning dress," she supplied.

Joanna nodded her thanks. "I have no details about their carriage, but the gentleman is in possession of a magnificent thoroughbred bay. There may also be a valet with them."

"There is," said the man with the whiskers.

Frederica took an involuntary step forward. "Are they here?"

"Alas, ma'am, no longer. They availed themselves of lunch and then drove away."

Disappointment surged through her, and she took herself to task. Joanna had been proved correct so far. She must hope she was correct in the other particulars.

The landlord examined Frederica's face. "You are like your sister," he concluded. Then, frowning, "Are they eloping?"

"If marriage were indeed the gentleman's aim, I would be more sanguine," said the Viscountess bluntly. "Ay, you may well look shocked, sir." She took five guineas from her reticule and pressed them on him. "You have already been most helpful. If there is anything more?"

He pocketed the money, his manner becoming subtly more deferential. "They are in a phaeton, ma'am. They left around three o'clock and seemed in no great hurry."

Joanna gave Frederica a significant glance. "Then they are not planning on reaching Dover tonight. They intend to put up somewhere on the road. That is good news indeed."

"Let us hope so," she murmured.

When it became clear that the landlord could offer little more in the way of information, they took their leave of him and made their way out of The King's Head. Joanne repossessed their refreshed horse and handed Frederica up into the dogcart.

"Courage, Frederica," urged the Viscountess, as she drove them back out onto the turnpike. "They will soon be within our sights."

DUSK WAS FALLING when they reached The White Hart, a prosperous coaching inn five miles further on. Joanna made Frederica wait in the dogcart while she enquired within. She emerged wearing a grim smile.

"Success. They are staying here under the name of Mr. and Mrs. John Smith." She grimaced at the false name. "Their valet is in a separate room."

Frederica leaped to her feet. "Joanna! Please help me down and take me to Amelia."

"I do not think it wise." The Viscountess reached for the box she had deposited on the dogcart's seat and, having taken one of the pistols from it, began to load the weapon.

Frederica was outraged. "But—"

"No buts, my dear. Lord Peregrine is dangerous, and the circumstances we find him in are bound to be indelicate. Even if you have no care for your reputation, I do. One sister ruined is quite enough."

"Joanna!"

"I mean it." The Viscountess turned on her such a forbidding look, she found herself meekly sitting back down. "You are here for one reason only, to take charge of your sister. Allow me to deal with the rest."

"Very well," she grumbled, conscious that their heated exchange was in danger of attracting attention.

"Thank you." Joanna softened her glare. "I will not betray your trust." She reached for her shawl and draped it over the pistol. "Wish me good fortune."

"I do. And please be careful," whispered Frederica.

The Viscountess gave her a small smile and walked away.

FREDERICA HAD NO idea how long she had been waiting— it seemed hours but was probably only minutes—when she heard a loud voice coming from The White Hart's stable.

"I know that bay horse, I tell you. It belongs to an old friend of mine." The words were slurred. "Won it in a bet. Damned close run thing it was too. But that's Perry for you."

She twisted round in her seat and watched as a man in a ribbed-silk evening tailcoat and ankle-length trousers, their colour indeterminate in the gathering darkness, emerged into the yard. A worried ostler was at his heels.

"You are mistaken, sir. A Mr. John Smith is the owner of that animal." The servant reached out his hand. "Sir, you cannot barge in on the gentleman and lady unannounced!"

"Who are you to tell me what I can and cannot do?" The drunken man shook off the servant's hand. "Stop pawing me, man. This coat's new, and your hands are filthy." He reeled across the yard, and Frederica shrank back in her seat. Luck was against her. He stopped beside the dogcart and gazed owlishly up at her.

"Good evening, ma'am. Name's Compton. At your service." He took off his top hat and bowed, almost falling over in the process. The ostler steadied him, and was shaken off for his pains. "Taking the air, are you, ma'am? And why not? It looks set to be a fine night." He sucked in an appreciative breath and promptly had a coughing fit.

"Please, sir," muttered the ostler, throwing Frederica an apologetic glance. "You are unwell. Let me assist you to your room."

Eventually Compton recovered his breath and straightened. "I am well enough." He seemed to have forgotten Frederica. "I must visit my old friend Perry." His eyes gleamed with merriment. "He has a lady with him? The rogue! I wonder who she is."

The ostler rolled his eyes. "For the hundredth time, sir, a Mr. Smith owns that horse."

"And for the hundredth time, I tell you, he is Lord Peregrine's. Now leave me in peace."

Hands twitching with frustration, the servant watched him stagger towards the coaching inn's entrance, then, muttering under his breath, returned to the stable. On impulse, Frederica jumped down from the dogcart and followed the drunken man indoors.

THE WHITE HART'S night porter was absent from his post, so it was a matter of moments for the inebriated man in the tailcoat to lean over the table, pull the visitor's book towards him, and scan its pages.

"John Smith. No. 17," muttered Compton. "Now where the deuce is that? Upstairs, I'll warrant. And knowing Perry, the best room in the place."

Chuckling to himself, he staggered towards the stairs, unaware of Frederica's presence a few paces behind him. She followed as silently as she could, using the shadows for cover. At the first landing, he hesitated, then shook his head and set off up the stairs once more.

One of the inn's patrons, a thin man in a caped overcoat, top hat, and cane, chose that moment to come down the stairs. He regarded Frederica frankly as he passed. She blushed and ducked her head and was relieved when he didn't accost her. Squashing an urge to retreat to the safety of the dogcart waiting unattended in the yard, she hurried on. The only thing that mattered was her sister's safety and reputation, and if this Compton fellow saw Amelia in Lord Peregrine's room . . . Goodness only knows what Joanna would say when she found out that Frederica had disobeyed instructions. But she would face that hurdle later.

"Aha!" came a slurred voice from the next landing. She was just in time to see her quarry setting off along the shadowy passageway.

Compton pressed his red nose to each door and peered short-sightedly at the numbers painted on it. Stopping at room 17, he shuffled his feet, chuckled to himself, and raised his fist. "Perry." He pounded on the door. "It's Compton here." *Bang bang.* "Mr. and Mrs. John Smith, eh? Coming it a bit strong! Can't fool me though. That nag is unmistakable." *Bang, bang bang.* "Come on, old fellow. Open up. Let's see this lady friend of yours. She's someone else's wife, I'll be bound."

All along the passageway, doors opened and the inn's patrons— some angry, some fearful—peered out. An old woman in a mobcap took one look at the drunken Compton and retreated, slamming the door closed.

Frederica could take no more. She darted forward.

"Please, sir." She curtseyed, keeping her head averted in the hope he would mistake her for a chambermaid. "You are disturbing our guests. Will you not return to your own room?"

"Know you, don't I?" Compton's fist paused, and he blinked at her.

"Come away, sir." She placed a hand on his arm, just as it occurred to him to do what he should have done in the first place—try the doorknob.

The door to Room 17 swung open with a creak, and Compton surged through it in triumph. "Aha!"

Frederica peered round his shoulder and started with dismay. Lying on the bed, half undressed, those few clothes they still wore unbuttoned and dishevelled, were Viscountess Norland and Lord Peregrine.

Joanna and Perry? Surely it couldn't be . . . She put a hand to her mouth. Much as she wanted to, she could not seem to turn away. Such kisses! They looked as if they were trying to devour one another. There was no sign of her sister.

The two on the bed broke off their embrace and turned annoyed glances Compton's way. Lord Peregrine was the first to speak.

"What the devil do you mean by interrupting us?"

"Who is this, Perry? Some friend of yours?" Joanna's expression was icy.

Compton began to shake with laughter. "Good God, 'tis Viscountess Norland! Perry, old fellow, I had no idea you and she—"

A feeling of nausea overtook Frederica. She turned and fled the scene.

IT WAS FORTUNATE that the horse had only wandered as far as the stable. It nickered at Frederica as she scrambled up into the dogcart and sat on the hard seat.

Her heart was pounding, and confusion made her head ache. She couldn't get the scene she had just witnessed out of her head. She supposed she should be pleased it had not come to a duel, but somehow it had been much worse to see the Viscountess and Lord Peregrine doing . . . that.

What a fool she had been!

The impulse to ride for home was strong, and she reached for the reins only to relinquish them again. Amelia. She could not leave without Amelia.

She hid her face in her hands. Trust her, Joanna had said. But was her sister even at The White Hart? She had blithely gone along with everything the Viscountess told her. But just suppose—

Footsteps approaching her in a hurry snagged her attention. She looked up angrily, expecting to see Joanna with some all too plausible excuse on her lips. But it was Amelia's tear-stained face gazing up at her.

"Oh, Frederica. I am so glad you have come. How could he send me away like that? He said he loved me."

"Amelia!" Relieved beyond measure, she jumped down and hugged her sister. "Are you well? Did he harm you?"

"Perry would never do anything I did not want him to," came her sister's muffled reply. "Everything was perfect until *she* turned up."

That wasn't quite what Frederica had asked but she bit her tongue. She released her hold and stepped back, the better to examine her sister's face. Amelia looked more angry than heartbroken, she decided, feeling her anxiety ease.

"Perry is the most diverting company—I don't know when I have laughed so much in my life," said Amelia. "I would have been mistress of Painswick House. Just think of all the balls I could have given! And you could have visited me, and we would have had a high old time." She blew her nose on a sodden handkerchief.

"How can you be so foolish?" Frederica resisted the urge to shake her sister. "Lord Peregrine would never have wed you, Amelia. He is penniless. He must marry money." Belatedly she wondered if even that was true. She had only Joanna's word for it, after all.

"That wouldn't have mattered, Frederica. He loved me, I am certain of it. I had just to be patient, and he would have married me in the end." Amelia's lips thinned. "And then *she* turned up. Oh! Why did she have to spoil everything?" She stamped her foot.

Frederica frowned. "But surely, it is better to know now that he loves the Viscountess than to discover it later?"

Her sister blinked. "That Perry loves *her*? Don't be such a goose! That was a sham for his friend's benefit. It's her *money* he loves. To think that he would allow her to buy him off for a paltry three hundred guineas!" Her face crumpled, and she began to cry once more.

Frederica handed her sister her own handkerchief and puzzled over what she had learned. There had been no sign of Amelia in Room 17, yet here she was. And how had she known Frederica was waiting in the dogcart unless Joanna had told her?

"Amelia, where were you when Mr. Compton burst in to Lord Peregrine's room?"

Her sister blew her nose. "The closet," she muttered.

"The closet!"

"Is that not insupportable? But I had no choice." Amelia's tone was indignant. "The Viscountess pushed me in. And she is so strong that willy-nilly in I must go. It stank of mothballs, Frederica. I thought I should choke on the stench!"

"The closet!" she repeated.

"Are you deaf?" asked her sister crossly. "It was that or under the bed. And I told her ladyship roundly what I thought of *that* idea." She turned and eyed the dogcart. "Could you not have chosen a more comfortable carriage, Frederica?"

"We chose for speed not comfort."

Amelia's eyes brightened. "You should have seen me in Perry's phaeton. I was the finest lady you ever did see."

Frederica didn't know whether to laugh or cry. Her mercurial sister had plainly taken no harm from her escapade. Her reputation was also intact. For which Joanna, if she had at last understood events correctly, was to be thanked.

She helped Amelia up into the dogcart. Her sister insisted on taking one of the front seats until it was pointed out to her that she would be sitting next to the Viscountess. This thought daunted her so much she settled on the rear-facing seat with scarcely a grumble. It couldn't last.

"It is getting quite chill. Must we wait for the Viscountess?" asked Amelia, after they had sat in silence for all of a minute. "Can you not drive us home, Frederica?"

"We must wait," she said shortly. "And while we do so, tell me everything that happened from the moment you left Chawleigh."

CHAPTER 10

"IT WILL BE all round London tomorrow, depend upon it," said Joanna, watching the drunken Compton depart and forcing herself not to dwell on the memory of Frederica's face. Shock, hurt, disgust. Those expressive eyes had betrayed the young woman's emotions all too clearly. If only she had done as she was told and waited in the dogcart.

"The two of us embracing in an inn on the Dover road?" Lord Peregrine gave his neckcloth a judicious twitch and buttoned up his waistcoat. "Of course. Who could resist such a juicy titbit?"

She reached for a shoe and slipped it on. "It seems I am still to be Notorious Norland, thanks to you."

He put on his coat and reached for the two rolls of banknotes she had given him. "A fellow has to live." He tossed them from hand to hand before pocketing them.

"At my expense." She couldn't keep the bitterness from her voice.

"You got off lightly, thanks to your friendly persuader." He gestured at the pistol lying on the bed. Pressed against his ribs, it had cut his demand substantially, besides preventing him from taking advantage of their staged embrace.

"Be thankful I didn't kill you."

A servant was passing their door, and Perry stopped him and asked him to send his valet to him. He turned back to her and smiled winningly. "Come with me, Joanna. We could have some good times. Just like the old days."

She threw him an exasperated glance. "When will you accept it? Those days are over. I am not who I was."

"Are you so sure?" He fingered his lips and smiled.

"Acting, my dear Perry. My feelings were not engaged."

"Neither were mine," he declared. But the flash of hurt in his eyes revealed otherwise.

She shook her head and paced over to the window. In the yard below, two lantern-silhouetted figures were sitting huddled in the dogcart. Night had fallen and the temperature was dropping. She would have to find them all rooms, but she had no intention of staying at The White Hart.

"They are waiting for me. I must go."

"To your Miss Bertram?" he said with a sneer.

"Ay. To her." She regarded him coolly. She now knew if she hadn't before that he belonged to her past not her present. "Goodbye, Perry. For old times' sake, I wish you well. But I devoutly hope I never see you again."

He assumed a mask of studied indifference. "As you wish." He straightened to his full height and bowed. "Goodbye, your ladyship."

Joanna curtseyed in response.

She was halfway down the passage when his voice floated after her. "But 'tis a shameful waste."

AN AWKWARD SILENCE held sway as the dogcart rumbled back along the turnpike towards The King's Head. Joanna glanced at the young woman sitting beside her. Frederica had scarcely looked at her let alone spoken to her since she climbed up into the dogcart and took the reins. She was either avoiding her, or preoccupied with something, and Joanna had a good idea with what.

She sighed and drove on. Five minutes further on, she noticed that Frederica had started to shiver.

"Are you cold?"

At the sound of her voice, Frederica started. "Indeed, I am beginning to feel the chill a little," came the quiet reply.

"A little!" cried Amelia from the rear seat. "Then you are fortunate indeed. I am like an icicle."

Frederica twisted round. "Oh, Amelia. Stop exaggerating."

"I am not."

"It cannot be much longer," soothed Joanna, flicking the reins. Five minutes later, the dim glow of lanterns appeared in the distance. "There is the coaching inn."

"At last," muttered Amelia.

Frederica was lost in her own thoughts again.

It was with relief that Joanna turned the dogcart into the King's Head's yard. She reined Chestnut to a halt and allowed the ostler to take charge of the horse and carriage while she ushered her shivering charges indoors.

The bewhiskered landlord greeted them all with a beaming smile and didn't bat an eyelid at their lack of luggage. "All is well again, ma'am?"

"As you see." Joanna ignored Amelia's curious glance.

She rented two good-sized rooms and requested that a light supper and some mulled wine be sent up. While a maid escorted the Bertram sisters to their room, she made her way farther up the passage to hers, where she was pleased to find a small fire burning in the grate.

After closing the door behind her, she flung herself on the bed. But as she lay, hands clasped behind her head, staring up at the ceiling and trying to clear her mind of the day's turmoil, she realised there was still one task to be undertaken. When the servant brought her supper, she asked him for paper, pen, ink, and sealing wax, which he returned with moments later.

Joanna wolfed down her food, barely noticing what it was, and spent the next half hour toasting her toes in front of the fire, sipping her mulled wine, and screwing up draft after draft of a letter to Mr. and Mrs. Bertram. Finally, the wording was to her liking, the hand reasonably legible with scarcely a single blot. With a satisfied grunt she waved the ink dry then folded and sealed the letter and impressed the cooling wax with her signet ring.

When a knock came at the door she thought it was the express messenger she had sent for.

"Come in."

The door creaked open, and a fair head peeped round it. "Am I disturbing you?"

"Frederica!" Joanna put down her letter and rose to her feet. "No. As you see." A thought struck her. "Is your sister unwell?" She slid her feet into her shoes.

"Oh no. She is sleeping soundly. The effects of a full stomach and the mulled wine, I daresay." Frederica shut the door behind her. "It is not on her behalf that I have come."

"Oh." Joanna resumed her seat and gestured Frederica to do likewise. "What did you wish to say to me?"

Frederica opened her mouth, but a knock at the door made her close it again.

"Come in," called Joanna.

It was the express messenger. She handed him the letter and gave him instructions about where to find Chawleigh House and who to give the letter to, stressed twice that he was to refuse payment, and pressed the correct sum into his hand, all the while conscious of Frederica's gaze.

When he had gone, Frederica regarded her with a smile. "How thoughtful of you to think of setting my parents' minds at ease and to defray their expenses," she said. "And how like you."

Joanna found herself blushing. She grabbed the poker and tended to the fire; perhaps Frederica would think she was merely hot. "Think nothing of it."

"I will not. When I think of what you have done for my sister today. For all my family, for we should surely have shared in Amelia's disgrace."

Joanna put the poker back in its rack and turned to face Frederica. "It was the least I could do, since it was by my offices that Perry met your sister in the first instance."

Frederica shook her head. "That will not do. You make light of it but I know what it cost you, Joanna. I gleaned the details from my sister and pieced them together. You paid him three hundred guineas from your own purse. Not only that, you sacrificed your own reputation so that my foolish sister's might be saved."

"You give me too much credit, my dear." Joanna had intended merely to buy Perry off. Sacrificing the reputation she had so recently begun to rebuild had not featured in her plan, but events had overtaken her, and what else could she do?

"I do not believe that." The admiration in Frederica's eyes was very agreeable.

"Well, well," said Joanna with a smile. "Have it your own way."

"And I am sure my parents will concur."

Joanna winced.

"What is wrong?"

"I fear your parents will hold a very different opinion, my dear, once my part in this affair appears in tomorrow's paper. Perry's drunken friend has a loose tongue and connections at the Gazette."

Frederica seemed dismayed but rallied quickly. "Then I will apprise them of the truth of the matter." Her brows drew together. "I am only sorry that you are to be subject to scandal on our account, Joanna. If only there were some way."

"There is not." She shrugged. "It doesn't signify, as long as those whose opinions I value still think well of me."

"I do." Frederica reached out and pressed her hand.

Joanna returned the pressure. "Thank you."

For a moment longer they held one another's gaze, then a yawn overtook Frederica.

"I do beg your pardon," she said.

Joanna laughed. "It is late, and we both need our rest. Tomorrow there is yet more travelling, and who knows what else?"

Frederica walked to the door. "Upon my word, I hope it is less eventful than today!"

"As do I." She regarded Frederica warmly. "Sleep well, my dear."

"You too, Joanna."

BUT JOANNA'S SLUMBERS were disturbed. For, though both women had avoided the subject of Chaloner Dunster's proposal of marriage, it coloured her dreams nonetheless.

Frederica, dressed all in white, was walking down the aisle towards the smiling Mr. Dunster. Joanna could only watch as they stood before the altar and took their solemn vows.

Then the scene changed, and she found herself, wearing riding clothes, kicking her old horse Conqueror into a gallop. She was chasing a phaeton, and the reason soon became clear. Frederica and her new husband were the carriage's occupants, with eyes for no one but each other. Joanna cried out to Frederica to wait for her, but if the other woman heard her she gave no sign.

No matter how fast she drove Conqueror, the carriage continued to draw away, until finally it disappeared over a hill into the distance.

CHAPTER 11

THE JOURNEY BACK to Chawleigh was passing far too quickly for Frederica's liking. It was a fine morning, and if she ignored Amelia's prattle from the rear seat of the dogcart, she could pretend she was out for a pleasant drive with Viscountess Norland. And she certainly had no wish to speed her meeting with Chaloner Dunster.

For the umpteenth time she glanced at the woman sitting quietly beside her. Joanna looked weary and rumpled and out of sorts, for all the attentions of the inn servant assigned to help them wash and dress. Frederica supposed she must look in similar condition. Though she had been almost dead on her feet when she took her leave of Joanna last night, wondering what she should say to Chaloner had kept her awake until the early hours.

It had not been easy, deciding what to do. The advantages of her match with Mr. Dunster were many and various. Her parents and neighbours would all welcome it, as would Chaloner himself—he wanted a mistress for his country house, and she would do as well as any. It would ensure she was comfortably settled for the rest of her life. And there would undoubtedly be children.

But weighed against that was her realisation that, in her hour of need, it was not to Chaloner that she had turned. Her first thought, on hearing of Amelia's disappearance, had been to seek help from the Viscountess. And her instinct had been sound—Joanna had proved more than equal to the task.

Would Chaloner have acted so quickly and resolutely to follow the eloping pair? More likely he would have hesitated, and by then they would have been in France, and Amelia's virtue lost for good. Would he have paid off Lord Peregrine from his own funds, or failing that challenged him to a duel? She did not think so. Chaloner favoured words over deeds and would have been helpless against a man as ruthless as Perry. More crucially still, would he have sacrificed his own reputation for Amelia's? Again, she thought not.

The dogcart came abreast of a signpost, and the Viscountess turned the horse towards Chawleigh saying, "Only ten miles now."

Frederica found herself staring at the Viscountess's profile, comparing it to Chaloner's. Joanna's high cheekbones, straight nose, and noble brow were the more striking, as were her eyes, which were of an infinitely preferable hue.

An enquiring glance from those same eyes made her blush and turn her gaze away. After she had managed to calm her beating heart, her thoughts resumed their unfavourable comparison of Chaloner to Joanna.

She was being unfair to him, she acknowledged. It would have been impossible for Chaloner to have known Perry's favourite haunts as Joanna did. As for realising that it was money Perry wanted rather than Amelia, he had not been friends with his lordship for years the way Joanna had. But this very unfairness was yet more evidence that she did not care for him. It would be only common decency to release him so that he might find someone better suited.

But if she did refuse his offer, if she relinquished her claim to be mistress of Symond Hall, what choices remained open to her? Spinsterhood? Clinically, she considered that state. Remaining a spinster was not such a very bad thing, surely, and better than marrying someone she did not love. As for children, acting the loving aunt to her nephews and nieces would satisfy that need. As long as she could see Joanna now and then.

She turned to regard her companion once more. "I hear you have rented a house close by. Murviton, is it not?"

Joanna gave her a tired smile. "Indeed. Have you visited the place?"

"No, but I would like to." She blushed as she realised how forward that sounded.

"It has a charming rose garden," said Joanna, apparently unaware of Frederica's gaffe. "The scent is astonishing. You would love it, I venture. You must come and visit. Amelia too, of course."

"That would be pleasant." Frederica chewed the inside of her lip. "When do you plan to set up residence there?"

"My plans are uncertain at present." She gave Frederica a rueful smile. "What of *yours*, Frederica? Have you decided what you will tell Mr. Dunster?"

She was acutely aware of Joanna's gaze and of Amelia's listening presence. But she could not bring herself to speak of her decision. For what if her courage failed her at the last, and she took the easy route and accepted Chaloner?

"I perfectly understand your reticence," said Joanna, breaking the awkward silence. "You quite naturally wish to discuss it with him first." She flicked the reins. "May I wish you every happiness, whatever your decision?"

"Thank you."

They rode the rest of the way in silence.

"AMELIA! FREDERICA!" THE front door had opened, and their mother was hurrying towards them before the dogcart came to a halt. "My dear girls! Are you *both* returned to me safe and sound after your ordeal?" Their father watched them from the doorway.

"We are well, Mama," called Frederica. "Thanks to Viscountess Norland."

Mrs. Bertram glared at Joanna and dropped a curtsey so reluctant it mortified Frederica. No greeting? No word of thanks, not even for the letter of reassurance the Viscountess had so thoughtfully sent by express mail? She felt ashamed of her mother. Could she but know how much their family owed to Joanna.

"Oh, Mama!" Amelia had been helped down from the carriage by a servant, and now threw herself against her mother's breast. "He would have married me eventually," she sobbed. "And I would have been mistress of Painswick House. If it had not been for the Viscountess . . ."

"There there, my dear." Their voices faded as they went indoors. Frederica's attention shifted to her father.

"I'm much obliged to you, your ladyship, for bringing my daughters safe home." Mr. Bertram bowed politely to the Viscountess, but his tone was frosty. "Come inside, Frederica. I am sure we have much to talk about."

The servant was waiting to help her down, but she hesitated. "Please accept my apologies for my family's ungracious behaviour," she murmured.

"It doesn't signify, my dear." Joanna's face was studiedly neutral. "No doubt your parents have seen this morning's Gazette and are merely reacting accordingly." She gestured towards the waiting servant. "Step down. The comforts of home await you, and I must return this carriage to my brother."

Reluctantly, Frederica allowed herself to be handed down.

"Goodbye, Miss Bertram," said the Viscountess.

The formal mode of address made Frederica turn and frown. Joanna had picked up the reins and was urging the horse into motion.

Something about the set of Joanna's shoulders made her give in to the impulse to call out, "I will come to Thornbury Park tomorrow morning to give Mr. Dunster my answer. Perhaps I will see you then?"

For a moment she thought Joanna had not heard her, then a gloved hand rose in acknowledgement.

With a small sigh of relief, Frederica watched the dogcart until it had turned out of the drive. Then she turned to her silently waiting father. "You have something to say to me, Papa?"

He nodded. "Come, my dear."

"YOU MUST BREAK your association with Viscountess Norland, Frederica." Mr. Bertram gestured at the newspaper lying open on his desk. "We agreed to give her the benefit of the doubt, but she has proved as disreputable as ever."

She opened her mouth to speak but his raised hand stopped her.

"I know she brought Amelia back safe, child. But if it had not been for her, that foolish girl would not have come into Lord Peregrine's sphere of influence in the first place." He shook his head. "How I can have raised daughters so level-headed as you and so empty-headed as Amelia escapes me. Though considering your mother's temperament, it should not. Perhaps it is as well you did not both turn out empty-headed."

She could contain herself no longer. "Papa! If you only knew the truth of what Joanna has done for us."

He blinked at her in astonishment. "Joanna is it?" Her cheeks grew warm. "Well, well," he said, after a short pause. "A judge must hear all sides of the case before pronouncing sentence. Perhaps you will tell me Joanna's side?"

So tell him she did, holding nothing back, and gesticulating wildly as she did so. At last she drew to a close. There was silence in the library apart from the ticking of the clock on the mantelpiece.

"Upon my word! Three hundred guineas, you say?" He sounded quite overcome. "And this"—he gestured at the paper—"a red herring to draw attention away from Amelia?"

She nodded.

"Well, well. That throws quite a different light on the matter." He rose and began to pace. "To find myself so indebted to the Viscountess." He halted and sighed. "I must repay her, of course."

"You may offer, but I daresay she will not take it." Frederica bit her lip. "Will you tell Mama the particulars? I cannot bear it that she was so rude to Joanna. She does not deserve such shabby treatment."

He smiled fondly at her. "You have always had a kind heart, my dear. And of course you want only what is best for your friends, among whose number you have clearly included Viscountess Norland. Well, I will try. But as you must know by now, your mother hears what she wants to hear."

"Even so."

He patted her hand. "I said I will try." He folded up the paper and set it aside. "Now, as to that other matter."

"Papa?"

"Your decision about Mr. Dunster. Have you made it yet?" He sat down, steepled his fingers, and regarded her with interest.

Her heart began to race, and she fiddled with her gloves while she decided how to proceed. "We have spoken of this before. I did not love Mr. Dunster then, Papa, and I do not love him now."

"But will you be happy as a spinster, my dear? Can you forego the pleasures of companionship, of children?"

"How can I know the answer to that? But I will try, with all my heart. For there are other forms of companionship than that of a husband, are there not, and there will always be my nephews and nieces to spoil."

"My dear girl." He stood up and came round his desk, his arms open wide. She leaned against his chest and let him embrace her, feeling the prick of tears against her eyelids. "I want only for you to be happy," he said. "If you must refuse Mr. Dunster to be so, then do it with my blessing."

"Thank you, Papa."

"But do not on any account let your mother know that I said so."

Laughter bubbled up inside her, pushing the tears away.

CHAPTER 12

IT WAS WITH a feeling of gloom that Joanna turned her brother's dogcart onto the gravelled drive leading to Thornbury Park. If the Bertrams had read that morning's copy of the Gazette, Edmund's household was likely to have seen it too. One thing was for certain. It was fortunate that she had rented Murviton, for it was a racing certainty that she would find herself taking up residence there sooner rather than later.

As she reined Chestnut to a halt in front of the entrance, Walter hurried out to greet her.

"Thank you." She stepped down and handed the footman the reins, before turning to gather up the walnut box that contained her pistols. "See that Chestnut is handsomely rewarded, will you? For he has done me great service these past twenty-four hours." At the mention of his name, Chestnut whinnied and shook his mane.

"As you wish, your ladyship."

Joanna watched Walter lead the horse and dogcart in the direction of the stables, then turned, took a deep breath, and went in. She had barely stepped across the threshold when her abigail came running towards her, face creased with anxiety.

"Is all well, your ladyship?" called Dorothea, when she was still some yards distant.

Joanna nodded. "Miss Bertram and her sister are safe returned to Chawleigh."

"Thank heavens." Dorothea pressed a hand to her breast with relief. Then her gaze sharpened. "And you, your ladyship. How goes it with you?"

"Ah, that is the question, is it not?" murmured Joanna. "I shall find out presently."

"Do those need cleaning?"

She followed Dorothea's gaze to the walnut box that contained her pistols. "If you mean did I have cause to discharge them, the answer is no."

"A pity," said Dorothea, accepting the heavy box from her. "For I cannot think of anyone who more sorely deserves a peppering than Lord Peregrine."

"On that we agree." Joanna handed her abigail her hat and gloves.

"Where is his lordship?"

"Gone."

"Good riddance," muttered Dorothea.

Footsteps made both women turn. Joanna's heart sank when she saw it was Chaloner Dunster, come to investigate. When he saw who it was, he threw Joanna a look of dislike. His gaze travelled past her, becoming one of puzzlement and frustration.

"Is Miss Bertram with you?"

"No, Mr. Dunster. She is at Chawleigh."

He frowned. "Has she concluded her urgent business?"

"Indeed I believe so, sir."

He turned on his heel as if to go, then turned back. "I feel bound to tell you," he began, provoking a sigh from Joanna, "that if Miss Bertram's reputation has been harmed by her association with you, I will—"

"What, Mr. Dunster?" she interrupted. "Withdraw your offer of marriage?"

His face grew red. "On the contrary. You may esteem me as little as I do you—"

"I doubt that is possible," she murmured.

"—but the proposal still stands. Miss Bertram will be grateful for it, I am certain. She cannot but be mindful that a match with a man of my probity and respectability will counteract any loss her own reputation may have sustained."

He had made no mention of feelings, either his own or Frederica's, noticed Joanna. It was a damned high price to pay for respectability! She was about to respond when Edmund's butler appeared.

"Mr. Lynton sends his respects, your ladyship. He is awaiting you in the library."

"Thank you. I will join my brother directly."

She beckoned her abigail closer and said in a low voice, "You had better pack our things."

Dorothea's eyebrows rose. "Another moonlight flit, your ladyship?"

"Ay. To Murviton."

"Very good." Dorothea curtseyed and hurried away.

With a curt nod to Chaloner, Joanna left him and made her way down the passage to the library.

Her brother got to his feet as she entered. He was alone, and on the table in front of him lay a copy of the Gazette. Joanna's heart sank. She squared her shoulders and closed the door behind her.

"Joanna." His manner towards her was stiff, his voice colourless. Not a good omen. He gestured to the chair opposite him.

"Edmund." She seated herself, folded her hands, and waited.

For a long moment the two siblings regarded one another, and she tried to interpret his expression.

"How fares Miss Amelia?"

"She is well," said Joanna. "And safe delivered with her sister to Chawleigh."

Some of the stiffness left him. "Then you reached her in time?"

She nodded. "I must thank you for the loan of Chestnut. For without him, I fear we would have arrived too late. You have an excellent hunter there, Edmund."

"I know." From his tone, his thoughts were elsewhere. His gaze fell on the Gazette and his brows drew together.

"Is it very scandalous?" she asked.

"You have not read the article in question?"

She shook her head. "Nor have I any wish to. I can imagine its contents all too well."

He studied her. "Lord Peregrine is bound for the Continent, apparently. And rumour has it that you are to join him there."

"Am I indeed? That is news to me."

Edmund smiled, and a knot inside her eased, as she perceived not anger and disgust but rather fondness mixed with perturbation. Evidently he knew his sister's heart and had put two and two together. It would have pained her if he had believed the worst.

He sighed. "Was there no other way, Joanna?"

"Than to ruin my reputation once more? There might have been had I but a little time to think, which alas I had not." She gave a regretful shrug. "It doesn't signify."

"I see." He rose and began to pace. "I suspect Miss Amelia is neither aware of your generosity nor appreciative of it, Joanna." They exchanged a rueful glance.

"She is young, Edmund. And foolish." Joanna's lips quirked. "Were we not all young and foolish once?"

"Spoken like a Dowager. And I was not so foolish as all that."

"*Touché.*"

He stopped pacing and turned to regard her. "Damn it, Joanna. Can you not see that your action has placed me in a quandary?"

"Indeed, I am leagues ahead of you. My abigail is packing as we speak."

He looked startled. "Is she?" He took his seat once more, his eyes sad. "You do not deserve this, Joanna. But Caroline—"

"You have told your wife of Amelia and Perry's elopement?"

"On the understanding she never tells another living soul, not even her brother."

"Thank you."

Edmund dismissed her thanks with a wave. "But as long as the world at large does not know the truth—"

"I am scandalous company," Joanna finished for him. "I understand perfectly. Caroline is only thinking of her children's welfare. And of yours." She pursed her lips. "Were I in her shoes, I would do the same."

Warmth filled his gaze. "How like you to say so, sister." He rubbed his forehead and went on apologetically, "It is hard on you, however. And grossly unjust."

She shrugged. "I made my bed, I must lie on it."

"Well." He examined a thumbnail. "We must look on the bright side. The scandal surrounding you will die down in time, and then you may safely resume our acquaintance. But until then—" He looked up.

"I must be circumspect. Of course." She kicked back the chair and stood up. "In that case, I had best take my leave of you without further ado, brother."

"This instant?" He blinked at her. "Where will you go?"

"To Murviton." She saw his incomprehension. "Ah! I have not had time to tell you. The afternoon of the elopement I was returning from placing a deposit on the place."

"But Murviton!" He blinked at her. "That is—"

"But a few miles from here." She nodded. "May I trouble for the loan of a gig, Edmund? For I have no time to rent my own. Oh. And some comestibles from your larder would be welcome."

He stood up, his expression one of vast relief. "Of course you may. You are my sister! Take anything you need."

THE KEYS TO Murviton House lay on the kitchen table, where Joanna had thrown them. Mr. Barton's eyes had almost bulged out of their sockets when she arrived on his doorstep unheralded, demanding to take possession of Murviton much sooner than anticipated. He had planned to air the house for her, he protested—dust lay thick on the dustsheets. She told him she did not care if the ceiling was falling down around her ears. He was in possession of her deposit, it followed therefore that she was entitled to the keys. At that, the house agent had handed them over.

A cook and menservants had yet to be engaged, so Joanna herself had stabled the gig Edmund loaned her and groomed and fed the horse. Dorothea was presently inspecting each musty room and compiling a list of necessaries to be purchased on the morrow. They had, for example, forgotten to bring any candles but fortune had smiled on them in the shape of some candle stubs hiding in a dresser drawer. At least they were not short of food and drink.

She carved herself another slice of the ham begged from Edmund's cook, tore off a handful of the loaf begged from the same source, and washed down her makeshift supper with a glass of the burgundy filched from Edmund's cellar, but her thoughts were elsewhere.

Joanna had shown her brother an insouciance she did not feel. And what had her grand gesture of quitting his house so promptly gained her? Just deserts indeed! For she would not be at Thornbury Park when Frederica arrived to give Mr. Chaloner her answer.

What would that be? She had once accused Frederica of being a pragmatist, she remembered with an inward wince. The pragmatic response of a young woman whose family had so recently escaped scandal by a whisker must surely be to accept his offer.

Frederica would be mistress of Symond Hall, and Chaloner would spirit her away to Norfolk. And Joanna would never set eyes on her again. That last thought was profoundly lowering.

"I found some blankets, your ladyship," said Dorothea, who had entered the kitchen unnoticed. "You should sleep tolerably well on that couch in the drawing room tonight and I—" She paused and put her hands on her hips. "What is this? A fit of the dismals will do neither you nor Miss Bertram any good."

Joanna's choler rose. "Upon my word, Dorothea! You go too far."

Dorothea's expression softened. "There," she said. "I'll take one of your temper tantrums over self pity any day."

"Self pity?" Joanna opened her mouth to protest before recognising the truth of the accusation. "How did you know I was thinking of Miss Bertram?" she asked crossly.

"It is as plain as the nose on your face."

Joanna touched her nose. "It is not all that plain, surely?"

Her abigail ignored the feeble attempt at humour, pulled out a chair, and helped herself to bread and ham. The kitchen fell silent except for the sounds of eating and the shifting of logs in the hearth. Joanna's gaze drifted to the window. Outside it was now full dark. A bat flittered past. She topped up her glass and sighed.

"You cannot blame Miss Bertram if she accepts Mr. Dunster's offer," said Dorothea, round a mouthful of bread and ham.

"Indeed I do not," said Joanna. "I have not the right."

"For she thinks she has no other choice."

Joanna threw her a testy glance. "You choose an odd way to lift my spirits, I must say!"

"Did it even cross your mind to *ask* her?" continued Dorothea, unperturbed.

"To ask her what, pray?"

"Has love dulled your wits? Why, to live with you here, of course." Dorothea helped herself to more ham.

Joanna stared at her abigail. "How could I? Miss Bertram is a respectable young woman, and I a . . . ." She trailed off.

A gleam appeared in Dorothea's eye, and Joanna silently dared her to complete the sentence. She did not disappoint. "Notorious libertine?"

Joanna refused to rise to the bait.

"But that is beside the point, your ladyship."

"There is a point?" asked Joanna, her tone dry.

Dorothea's lips twitched. "Ay. And it is that *you* are the one in a position to make such an offer whereas Miss Bertram is not." She reached for the wine bottle then paused. Joanna waved her permission.

"How could I ask such a thing of her?" she said, an edge to her voice. "It would expose her to scandal and opprobrium, and I would spare her that."

Dorothea sipped her wine. "Your brother keeps a good cellar!" she murmured with a look of pleased surprise, before adding, almost as an afterthought, "Does the world heap opprobrium on ladies' companions?"

It was a moment before a thunderstruck Joanna could catch her breath. To be a lady's companion was indeed a perfectly respectable occupation for a young woman of genteel birth with no other means of support. And any scandal attaching to Joanna could not reasonably be placed at her companion's door. Indeed, the unfortunate woman who found herself, through no fault of her own, in such a position would be more likely to receive sympathy than condemnation. And if unwanted pity and solicitous remarks became irksome, Frederica, she suspected, was of strong enough character to shrug them off.

"Why did not *I* think of that?"

"As I said," said Dorothea, "your wits have been very dulled of late."

"Hold your tongue," said Joanna, out of habit, for her thoughts were elsewhere. She allowed herself a daydream—walking hand in hand with Frederica in the rose garden on a sunny day. Then reality returned with a jolt.

There was no time to lose. She must ride to Chawleigh at once. She pulled out her pocket watch and glanced at it, then let out a curse. And disturb the whole household by pounding on the front door and demanding admittance at this time of night? Who could not but be alarmed by such wild behaviour? First thing in the morning then. A moment's reflection, however, convinced her that the outcome would be the same. For after that article in the Gazette, Mr. and Mrs. Bertram would surely not let Notorious Norland anywhere near their daughter.

"I fear I have left it too late," she said. Dejection returned.

"Back to self pity, are we?" Dorothea tutted. "Since when did you lower the flag so quickly?"

When indeed?

"You are right to chide me," said Joanna, forcing a smile. "For all is not lost until Miss Bertram has accepted Mr. Dunster's offer. And that I will learn tomorrow morning from her own lips." She took a breath and let it out. "In the meantime, there are other matters to attend to. You have finished your survey of the rooms and made a list of necessities to be purchased, I take it?"

Dorothea gave her an approving smile. "Indeed I have, your ladyship." She dug in the pocket of her skirt and produced a piece of paper. "It is rather on the lengthy side, I fear."

CHAPTER 13

FREDERICA WALKED DOWN the drive from Thornbury Park. Things had started out that morning well enough. Edmund Lynton had greeted her warmly on her arrival and asked after Amelia's health and her own. Then he had ushered her into the drawing room where Chaloner was eagerly awaiting her. From that point on, things had gone rapidly downhill.

To say Chaloner was displeased with her refusal was to put it mildly. At first he had thought she was joking. When it became clear she wasn't, he became by turns confused, disbelieving, and hurt. Finally had come real anger. She had never seen him angry before, and to think that she had been the cause of it gave her real pain. He had given her a stiff bow and a cold look and stalked off to his chamber. Then she had let herself out, only to run into Mr. and Mrs. Lynton. Caroline had learned of her brother's treatment, and she too turned cold towards her. Edmund looked merely disappointed.

As for Joanna, the one person she could have expected to take her side was unavailable. "The Viscountess is no longer in residence," said a servant, much to her dismay.

Frederica twirled her reticule and castigated herself as she walked. Who did she think she was, turning down the position of Mrs. Dunster just because it went against her inclination? Angry tears came to her eyes. "Foolish girl! Now what will become of you?"

The sound of hoofbeats made her look up. A rider was coming towards her, but she could not make out who it was. The horse was no thoroughbred but an animal more used to pulling a carriage by the look of him. She dashed the tears from her eyes and looked again.

Viscountess Norland was wearing breeches and sitting astride. Male attire suited her, decided Frederica, staring as the other woman reined her horse in, dismounted, and hurried towards her.

"Frederica." Joanna's demeanour was uncharacteristically anxious. Frederica wondered what was troubling her. "Have you paid your visit to Thornbury Park?"

She nodded. Her reply seemed to take the Viscountess by surprise. She surveyed their surroundings, as if searching for someone else, then regarded Frederica again in puzzlement.

"You are alone?"

Again Frederica nodded. This time her answer seemed to please the Viscountess. Her brows smoothed, and her manner became animated.

"Am I to understand from this that you have refused Mr. Dunster? For if you had just accepted *my* proposal, I would not leave you alone."

Frederica felt suddenly indignant. "I cannot see that that is any of your business," she said tartly.

A radiant smile lit up the Viscountess's face. "But you do not deny it. Good."

"Good?"

"I was afraid you would accept him. I am glad you did not."

Frederica blinked. Being with the Viscountess was always disconcerting, and this occasion looked like being no exception. She contented herself with a weak, "Oh."

Joanna grabbed her horse's reins and fell into step beside Frederica as they walked.

"I do not know why you should be glad," said Frederica, trying not to sound petulant. "I would have been mistress of Symond Hall. What is to become of me now?"

"He was not right for you."

"Who are you to say who is or is not right for me?"

Joanna merely laughed, and Frederica stared at her.

"Does my distress please you?"

"You would have me appear heartless, but truly I am not," said Joanna. "For I do not believe you are unduly distressed."

Frederica frowned. "You presume a great deal!"

"I do." Joanna glanced at her. "I have been thinking," she went on. "Or rather, Dorothea, my abigail, has—for as she delights in informing me, my wits have been sadly addled of late." That fact seemed to amuse her for some reason. "I believe I have found the solution to both your predicament and mine."

Frederica halted and turned to face her. "And what predicament is that, pray?"

"That we are both destined to be old maids."

"That is to be *my* fate, I agree, but *you* are married with a child and so cannot be a maid. And besides, I have heard you need never lack for company if you desire it." She was gabbling, she realised. Why did Joanna's company always affect her in this manner?

The Viscountess's smile widened. "I do believe you are being indelicate." She wagged a finger in mock disapproval.

Frederica blushed and wondered what had come over her. "And I believe you are being excessively provoking!"

Joanna let out a snort of amusement. "Your pardon, my dear. I will come to the point." She took Frederica's hand and refused to release it, though in truth Frederica did not try very hard to free herself. "No, my dear. Be still and listen. I came here this morning with the express purpose of asking you to live with me at Murviton. As my companion," she added, before Frederica could formulate the question.

"Your companion?"

"Yes," said Joanna, her expression teasing once more. "You have heard of such a thing?"

"Of course." The sudden change in her prospects made Frederica feel quite giddy. "A poor relation doomed to be at the beck and call of her rich employer," she said, "to placate her every whim."

Joanna's eyes danced. "I could not have put it better myself. Whim is a good word, an accurate word. I am determined to have lots of whims."

Frederica tried not to smile. "You think a good deal of yourself, your ladyship."

"Joanna, please. And can you deny that you enjoy my company?"

Frederica did not have to think. "No, I cannot deny it," she said.

"As I enjoy yours."

"Do you?"

A dark eyebrow rose. "Can you not tell?"

"I think you enjoy making sport of me," said Frederica.

"I do. And for that I apologise." Joanna pressed her hand. "Will you think about my offer, my dear? It is seriously meant." Her expression was as grave as Frederica had ever seen it.

"I have never had so attractive an offer, Joanna," said Frederica frankly. "But this is a momentous decision. I must talk to my father."

"Of course. Take as long as you like. Discuss it with whomsoever you like. Consult the soothsayers, toss a coin, pull petals from daisies. As long as in the end your answer is yes."

Frederica laughed. She had never seen the Viscountess in such a giddy mood. "And what if I say no?"

Joanna's hand waved in airy dismissal. "Then I will repeat my offer at regular intervals, until at last you grow tired of resisting me and say yes."

Frederica could not but feel flattered by such a remark. "You are very persistent."

A smile played around Joanna's lips. "It is my middle name."

"I thought that was Notorious."

"*Touché*," said Joanna. "But from now on it is Persistent."

Blue eyes held Frederica's, and she saw something in Joanna's expression that she had not seen in Chaloner's—warmth and honest affection. Her doubts disappeared, and what had for weeks seemed a decision fraught with difficulty was suddenly simplicity itself.

"I will talk to my father," she said. "And I will say yes."

EPILOGUE

JOANNA WAS RETURNING from walking the two golden retrievers Frederica had allowed her, after much persuasion, to purchase, when she saw her abigail hurrying out of Murviton's back door to intercept her.

"What is it, Dorothea?" she called.

"Miss Bertram's parents have arrived earlier than expected." The red-faced abigail came to a halt in front of her and pressed a hand to her side while she regained her breath. "And they have brought Mr. and Mrs. Dunster with them."

"Have they, by God!" Joanna pursed her lips. "How does Amelia look?"

"As you would imagine, your ladyship—insufferably pleased to be the new mistress of Symond Hall. I daresay she will pull rank over her sister at dinner."

"Knowing Frederica, she will be happy to let her."

Joanna whistled the dogs to heel. Cowper obeyed instantly, but Sefton had to be called twice. "Has Cook been informed we have guests for dinner?"

Dorothea nodded. "It is all in hand."

"Good. Where are they now?"

"Miss Bertram is entertaining them in the drawing room. She requests you to join her as soon as is convenient and," the abigail hesitated before continuing delicately, "suggests you wear a dress."

Joanna let out a bark of laughter. "Does she indeed? Very well, tell her I will be there as soon as I have changed, then attend me in my chamber."

"Very good, your ladyship." Dorothea curtseyed and hurried away.

Joanna gave the dogs into the care of a footman, tugged off her boots—Frederica took exception to having mud tracked over their carpets—and climbed the stairs to their chamber. Dorothea had already selected and laid out a blue satin afternoon dress, with shoes and gloves of a lighter shade. She stripped off her coat, waistcoat, and shirt, peeled off her breeches, and allowed Dorothea to button her into her new attire.

There was no time to do anything much with her hair, so her abigail, tutting throughout, swept it back into a bun at the nape of her neck. A last check in the mirror satisfied her she would not shame Frederica, then she set off downstairs.

Frederica was pouring milk into china cups when Joanna entered the drawing room, and she threw her a look of pure relief. Joanna grinned and, after greeting their guests, went at once to her side.

"Is this dress to your liking?"

Frederica appraised her. "Blue becomes you. Thank you, Joanna. I know it must be tiresome for you."

"The pleasure is mine. Are they behaving themselves?"

"Father is bored out of his wits, mother thinks we should buy new curtains as these are horrendously faded and old-fashioned, and Amelia is acting as if she is royalty rather than plain old Mrs. Dunster." She put down the milk jug and reached for the silver teapot. "As for Chaloner, he has been showing off dreadfully. I think he is trying to make me realise what I missed, but I am already acutely aware of it and grateful beyond measure for my narrow escape."

Joanna laughed. "If only he knew that he has you to thank for throwing Amelia in his path."

"Shhh!" Frederica looked round, but their guests were talking amongst themselves and had not heard Joanna's remark. "Well," she continued in a low voice, "they *are* much better suited. For she is pretty and silly, and already as obsessed with Symond Hall as he is. And he is much richer and handsomer than Herbert Smith ever was."

"A perfect match."

"You are joking, but I believe it truly is, Joanna. Even better, now she has landed Chaloner, Amelia never mentions Lord Peregrine, whereas once he was the subject of every other sentence."

"A blessing indeed!"

"There, the tea is poured." Frederica put down the teapot and reached for the heavy tray, but Joanna beat her to it.

"Allow me." A quick press of her hand was her reward.

They joined their guests on the sofa, Joanna placing the tray on a convenient table, and Frederica passing out the cups of tea. And if the newly wed Mr. and Mrs. Dunster were surprised to be offered the sugar bowl and tongs by a Viscountess—Joanna never stood on ceremony in her own house—they hid it well.

The afternoon passed into evening in talk and laughter and exchanges of glances between Joanna and Frederica. The Dunsters were full of their recent honeymoon in Sussex—they had stopped off in Kent on their way back to Norfolk—and their plans for Symond Hall. Mrs. Bertram's excessive admiration of everything they said grew tiresome, but Joanna resolved to be patient for Frederica's sake. As for Mr. Bertram, his opinion seemed to be similar to her own, for he too bit his lip from time to time, and whenever his gaze fell on his eldest daughter, a gentle smile curved his lips.

"My daughter is looking very well, your ladyship," he remarked when they had a moment to themselves—Frederica was playing the pianoforte Joanna had had installed for her, and Amelia was turning the pages.

"Indeed she is."

"When first she told me you had asked her to be your companion I had my doubts," he confided. "But she was confident you would make her happy so I could not deny her. She has been proved correct, I venture. And for that I thank you."

"No need," she said gruffly. "For I have got as much and more from our bargain. She has turned Murviton from a house into a home—something I had not realised I missed so badly until I had it once more."

"Nevertheless." He smiled and changed the subject. "How are those dogs of yours? Answering to your commands yet? Frederica tells me you have named them after two of the patronesses of Almack's."

Joanna grinned and nodded. "I am not above taking petty revenge, I fear. For the ladies of the committee barred me from admittance." She arched an eyebrow at him and said in a meaningful tone, "My supposed tryst with Lord Peregrine."

"Ah."

"Not that I mind on my own behalf," she went on. "For their balls, though exclusive, are insipid affairs. But I would have liked to show Frederica the assembly rooms."

He glanced at his daughter. "I do not think she will mind overmuch."

She followed his gaze. "Nor I. But it would have been pleasant to have the opportunity when next we are in town." She paused. "But you were asking about the dogs, Mr. Bertram. Cowper is coming along tolerably well. Sefton still has his own ideas."

Later, after a hearty dinner during which Amelia did indeed claim precedence over her unmarried sister, Joanna and Frederica waved off their guests in their carriages, directed the servants to lock up, and retired to their chamber.

Joanna helped Frederica out of her dress, stays, chemise, and petticoat, then set to work on garters and stockings. "It went well, did it not?" She ran a finger down a bare leg, receiving part yelp part giggle for her pains.

"Apart from the drawing room curtains, which I do not think my mother will ever like." Frederica instructed her to turn round and began unbuttoning Joanna's dress.

"Faded and old-fashioned indeed!" Joanna looked over her shoulder. "She should have seen my Paris house. Dorothea continues to upbraid me for the cockroaches."

Frederica pretended to shudder. "I trust you will never expect *me* to stay in such a place."

"No indeed." A kiss on her shoulder signalled Frederica was done.

Joanna let her dress pool round her ankles, flung her undone stays aside, and pulled the chemise over her head. While she was at her most vulnerable, Frederica tickled her ribs. In her efforts to avoid her tormentor, Joanna ripped the seam of her dress.

"Now look what I have done!" she complained. "Dorothea will nag me for days."

The hangdog expression she assumed merely made Frederica laugh harder.

"If the curtains are old-fashioned, they merely match the rest of Murviton," continued Joanna, resuming their earlier conversation, "which I would class rather as comfortable. Indeed comfort was one of its chief attractions, that and the rose garden and the fact it was so near to Chawleigh."

"You have certainly made me feel very comfortable here," said Frederica, smiling and stepping out of her drawers

"I'm happy to hear it." Joanna reached for the nightgown Dorothea had laid out for her. But the shake of a fair head told her it was not required, so she grinned and flung it across the room.

Frederica's own nightgown soon followed, and she slipped into bed. "I think my father approves of you."

Joanna slid in beside her and pulled her close. "If he saw us now, he would sing a different song."

"Let us thank the Lord he cannot." Frederica pulled Joanna's head down and kissed her, and Joanna took a moment to marvel at the changes eight months had wrought.

They had begun their new life at Murviton as particular friends, though the world thought them mistress and companion. But as she had hoped, friendship had deepened into something else.

Joanna had taken things cautiously, but Frederica showed no signs of repulsing her advances, indeed she seemed to welcome them. In the early days she was like a young colt, skittish and ready to bolt should Joanna's kisses and caresses stray too far beyond the bounds of propriety. But gradually her confidence grew, and she showed signs of relishing Joanna's increasingly bold touches.

The night she finally coaxed Frederica into her bed had been exhilarating. Under Joanna's patient tuition, and with the aid of a glass or two of madeira, Frederica's trepidation and reserve had vanished like morning mist, to be replaced by a sensual abandon hitherto unsuspected. Such an ardent response had astonished Frederica almost as much as it gratified Joanna. And as the hands roaming over her now indicated, Frederica had insisted Joanna ravish her as frequently as possible ever since.

She returned her thoughts to the here and now and began returning the caresses, to Frederica's evident delight. Afterwards, they flopped back onto the pillows, the sleepy young woman cradled in Joanna's arms.

Joanna formed the sheets and blankets into a cocoon around them both. "What shall we do tomorrow?" she murmured in a delicate ear. "Edmund has invited us to dine, but we need not go if there is something else you would prefer." Relations between their households had warmed considerably since Chaloner transferred his attentions to Amelia.

Frederica gave a languid stretch that reminded Joanna of a sated cat and yawned. "I care not." She traced the scar on Joanna's shoulder then stroked her cheek and snuggled closer. "Though it is not yet the time of year for it, even haymaking would be acceptable, if I could but do it with you beside me."

Joanna smiled in the darkness. "Then I shall make certain to be always beside you, my love."

Her answer was a soft snore.

The Adventures
of
Murdering Meg

1

A PIRATE'S TREASURE

MARGARET ETHEREGE SNAPPED her fingers. "A glass, prithee, Mr. Mostyn." The quartermaster slapped the spyglass into her open palm, and she extended the instrument and raised it to her eye.

The smudge on the horizon sprang into sharp focus, and she sighed with relief at the sight. There in the lens was a brigantine in full sail, a red flag with the cross of St. George in one corner fluttering from her mainmast. From her course, she must have left Jamaica two days ago, headed northeast up the Windward Passage, and was almost certainly bound for England.

"Is it the *Bristol*?" asked Mostyn.

"Ay. She's flying the Red Ensign, and she's right where she's meant to be." Meg turned to regard the eager faces of her crew. "There's our prey, lads. And if my informant is correct, her hold is full of silver and gold, rubies and diamonds."

Most of the men cheered, but one man's brow creased. "She's flying British colours, Captain. Shall we not be risking our Letter of Marque by attacking her?"

Meg pursed her lips and gave the young sailor with the beaky nose a grudging nod. Plague take it! Killigrew was frequently a boil on her backside, but he had a point. Normally they restricted themselves to Spanish prey. Attacking one of their own countrymen was a different matter.

"Strike our colours," she told Mostyn. "Run up the black flag instead. The Governor won't be able to revoke our commission on those grounds at least."

The quartermaster nodded and gave the order. The now sombre crew watched in silence as a plain black flag replaced their own Red

Ensign. Now they were no more than common pirates, stripped of even the pretence that they were working for the Crown.

"Take heart, lads." She gave them a broad grin. "Murdering Meg will get you through this encounter in one piece. And you'll be richer by the end of it."

As she had calculated, the use of her nickname and mention of money raised her men's spirits. And, hopefully, keeping busy would keep the rest of their qualms at bay.

Meg turned to the sailing master, waiting patiently beside the helm for her order. "Your best speed, Mr. Coke. I'll have that ship's treasure in our hold by dusk tonight or know the reason why."

"Ay, Captain." Coke began gesturing and yelling orders, and sailors ran to man the ropes or rushed barefoot up the rigging.

Absently, she buttoned up her doublet and watched the topsails unfurl before bellying out as the wind caught them. The *Kestrel* increased her speed perceptibly, and she grunted in satisfaction. This time of year, the trade winds shifted slightly to the north, blowing strongly toward the Bahamas. To make any headway back to England, a ship's fore and aft sails must be set just so, and frequent tacking was the order of the day. But she need have no worries on that score while Henry Coke was at the helm. If the wind didn't drop, they should catch their prey before nightfall. But if it did . . .

She squashed that thought at once, relaxed her shoulders, and trained her glass on the distant ship once more. A wry smile creased her lips when she realised she was subconsciously willing the *Kestrel* closer to its prey. As if that would make any difference.

In terms of cannon, hunter and prey were equal—six guns apiece, if her information was correct. But what the captain of the fleeing brigantine could have no way of knowing was that accompanying Meg was Woodes Read, the best master gunner she had ever sailed with.

She lowered the glass and winked at a passing sailor. He blushed and hurried on.

"Are you certain of this course, Meg?"

Mostyn had come up beside her. His voice was low, his address informal. She nodded her thanks for not questioning her judgement in front of the crew.

"Ay. For five years I've been searching for a way to repay Thomas Digges. If my informant is correct, there is treasure on board that ship, and by hook or by crook I mean to get it." Yet she had so nearly missed the chance she had been waiting for. Had news of the *Bristol*'s cargo not reached her ears during that brief visit to the tavern in Port Royal . . . She shivered, and it wasn't the spray driving off the ocean that had caused the chill.

"Digges. Did he not . . . ?" The quartermaster's voice trailed off.

"Ay," growled Meg. "That whoreson gave me the pretty scars on my back. Devil take him and his villainous offspring!"

The mere thought of what the sugar plantation owner and his sons had done to her made her stomach roil. Even now she had nightmares about the flogging and what had come after. Mostyn waited, his silence tacit invitation to confide, but as always she declined. She had served with him for three years, proving herself the equal of other pirates, working her way up through the ranks, and counted him her closest friend. But telling him about the scars on her back had been one thing, her other more invisible scars must remain so.

The quartermaster sighed, breaking the silence first. He had always been good that way. "I pray 'tis a valuable haul, Captain." She noted his return to formality with relief. "Nothing irks the men more than the risk outweighing the spoils."

"On my head be it. But it will be rich pickings, I wager." She gave him a crooked smile. "The *Bristol* is carrying Digges' daughter and her dowry. Her marriage contract is to seal an undertaking between Digges and a business acquaintance back in England."

Mostyn whistled through his teeth. "That's the song that little bird in *The Black Dogg* sang in your ear, eh?"

"Ay," she said dryly. "A little bird with a cursed large appetite for *reales*."

The wind freshened, and the *Kestrel* surged forward like a long-stabled colt sighting open meadow at last. Meg raised her glass once more and gazed at the distant ship. It was piling on more sail; its lookouts must have sighted them. Its Captain must be hoping to outdistance the pursuing brigantine, but the Trade Winds were against them both, and he had reckoned without the skill of Henry Coke.

THE *KESTREL* CAUGHT up with the *Bristol* just before dusk. The cannons facing the pirate ship were at last out of action, though for a while it had been touch and go.

There had been casualties during the exchange of fire. The *Kestrel* lost her aft sail and two men overboard with it—fortunately, Meg always insisted any man who sailed with her learn to swim, so they re-emerged, safe but dripping. A cannon crew were less fortunate. A lucky shot from the *Bristol* destroyed their gun, the resulting explosion and gout of flame burning five men beyond recognition and certainly beyond all hope of saving, even by Surgeon Avery's skilled hands.

Meg would get Mostyn to send the dead pirates' share of the plunder to their grieving wives and families, but she expected it was the whores in Port Royal and Tortuga who would miss them the most.

Coke had done his part, but it was her master gunner who finally brought the fleeing ship to heel. Read lashed the brigantine's rigging and sails with chainshot and brought down the *Bristol*'s mainmast with a single spectacular shot. Loud whoops and cheers greeted his success. Meg winced and hoped the passengers were safely below decks.

After that, the outcome of the battle was inevitable, though the crew of the now-drifting brigantine were determined not to go quietly, judging by the musket balls still peppering the *Kestrel*'s decks and puncturing her canvas.

There had been enough death and destruction, decided Meg. She despatched a quarter boat with instructions to row secretly round to the far side of the *Bristol* and board there, and ordered her men to prepare stinkpots.

As the gap between the two ships narrowed, she raised her cutlass and made a slashing gesture. At her signal, the pirates lit the pots' fuses and lobbed them onto the other ship. Foul-smelling black clouds obscured the wide-eyed faces of their opponents and wisps of the rank smoke drifted across the gap. The pirates held their noses and made uncomplimentary comments. From the other ship came sounds of choking and cursing. The rain of musket balls lessened noticeably.

"Grappling irons," she called.

The pirates crowding the rail threw the irons they had been gripping, and the sounds of metal thudding into wood filled the air. Meg's cheek stung. She pulled out a splinter with bloodstained fingers and flicked it away, then returned to watching her men work. Once the hooks were secure, brawny arms hauled on the thick ropes attached to them, bringing the two ships inch by inexorable inch closer together.

It was time. Meg leaped up onto the rail, grabbed the rigging to steady herself, then turned and bellowed at the members of the boarding party awaiting her command.

"Mark me well. Any man who breaks the Articles—especially Article 10—will answer for it. I tell you now, the punishment is DEATH!"

Those pirates who knew what she was talking about mouthed "no women" to those who didn't. Satisfied that she had damped down their lust a little at least, Meg took her cutlass in one hand, and leaped for the other ship's rail. She made it with ease, got her balance back, and pulled a flintlock from her belt. Then she twisted round and yelled, "*Kestrel*. To me."

With a bloodcurdling roar, the boarding party followed her.

THOUGH THE FOUL smoke from the stinkpots had cleared, soot-stained sailors lay curled up on the *Bristol*'s deck, some trying to catch their breath, the remainder heaving up the contents of their stomachs. Meg stepped round them, placing her boots with care and trying not to gag at the stench.

The temporarily disabled sailors paled even further when they saw who it was they faced. This raven-haired female pirate wearing male attire could be none other than Murdering Meg, Terror of the Spanish Main. There was a kernel of truth in the wild tales she encouraged her men to spread, but they didn't need to know how small it was.

They did the only thing they could in the circumstances, threw down their arms and begged for mercy. Smiling, she granted their request.

Meg detailed five pirates to gather up the weapons and stand guard, and sent Mostyn and fifteen others forward to get the transfer of loot from the hold underway. She beckoned the three remaining members of the boarding party to come with her and picked her way aft to where the sound of pistol fire and the clash of swords indicated fighting was still in progress.

It was hard going. The deck was slippery with blood and gunpowder, blocked by massive pieces of splintered mast and spar with the frayed remnants of canvas and rigging still attached.

The sounds of clashing blades grew louder. Up ahead was the hatchway to the passenger quarters. If Meg were Captain, that was where she would make her stand, protecting the passengers. Sure enough, when she rounded a corner, she saw a knot of six sailors defending the closed hatchway, and standing at their centre a tall, fair-haired man, whose expensively cut doublet and breeches looked the worse for recent fighting.

Three pirates who had crewed the quarter boat lay dead or groaning on the deck nearby. Only Killigrew and a pirate called Macrae were still standing, and they had exhausted their flintlocks and were using cutlasses. A discarded blunderbuss and several muskets showed the defenders were likewise reduced by lack of ammunition to using their blades.

Meg raised her flintlock to shoot the Captain cleanly through the heart then changed her mind. She fired into the air instead and jammed the now useless weapon back in her belt. Macrae and Killigrew turned grimy faces in her direction and grinned with relief as the three men with her hurried to join them. The odds were even now, and for a moment the two sides simply stared at one another.

The quickest way to end this, Meg knew, was for the fair-haired Captain to surrender his ship, but his face had twisted with disgust at the sight of her, and she doubted whether an appeal to his better nature would work. Unfortunately, this was one occasion where notoriety would work against her. Her bloodied cheek and the avid gleam in her eye couldn't be helping . . .

She raised her cutlass and stepped forward. "Stand back, lads. This is between the *Bristol*'s Captain and me."

Her men stood back, leaving the way clear. For a moment, she thought the opposing sailors weren't going to do the same, then their Captain nodded, and they too stepped aside.

"Winner takes all?" She raised an eyebrow in query.

He spat, the gob of spittle landing on the deck beside her boot. "A plague on you and all your kind!"

"You dress well, but your manners leave much to be desired, sir."

As they closed, the clash of his blade on hers sent a shock up her arm. He was strong, she realised, but then so was she, and they were of a height. More problematic was the fact that he was wielding a sword not a cutlass, with two edges and a longer reach. She darted a rueful glance at the slice that had appeared on her forearm and the blood beginning to stain her favourite shirt, and redoubled her efforts.

The trick was to keep her opponent close, so his sword's longer reach would be a hindrance not a help. After several minutes of slashing and parrying, she managed to get under his guard, and slash him in the side. It was only a shallow wound but it made him falter. When they closed once more, his grey eyes held more respect.

"Surrender your ship, and I will not harm your passengers," she told him, panting with effort and trying not to skid on the wood splinters, dust, and blood that seemed to coat everything. "My word on it."

He slashed at her thigh, but the tip of his blade snagged in the bucket-top of her boot, and she sidestepped quickly.

He evaded her thrust. "What good is a pirate's word?"

"For the love of God, sir, will you not listen?"

His heel came down in a smear of gore, and the resulting slip momentarily distracted him. Now was her chance. She slammed the hilt of her cutlass into his temple. Shock registered in his eyes, and his legs buckled. His men surged forward, but the pirates managed to keep them back.

Bringing all her weight to bear on her cutlass, she forced the other Captain's sword down and him along with it. "My word is as good as yours, I'll wager."

"The Devil take you!"

As the Captain of the *Bristol* struggled to free himself, she hooked her foot behind his calf and pulled. Unbalanced, he fell, in the process losing his grip. He hit the deck with a thud, rolled over, and looked round wildly for his sword. His fingers had just closed around it when she stamped on his wrist, feeling the crunch of bones. He cried out and let go.

She kicked the discarded weapon aside and pressed her blade to his throat. "Do you surrender?"

He blinked up at her in surprise. He had clearly been expecting a swift death. A long moment passed then his head dropped and his voice when it came was barely audible. "Ay. The ship is yours, madam. Captain James Bracegirdle, at your service."

"I am overjoyed to hear it, sir." She removed her foot from his wrist. "Captain Margaret Etherege, at yours."

She held out a hand. For a moment she thought he was going to refuse, then he clasped it and pulled himself up. The pirates, meanwhile, had relieved his dejected men of their weapons. Bracegirdle, cradling his injured wrist, went to join them.

"Macrae, Killigrew," said Meg, "with me. The rest of you take our prisoners to join their fellows."

"Ay, Captain," chorused her men.

As he was shepherded away, Captain Bracegirdle paused and looked back at her, his gaze shadowed. "Now we shall see what a pirate's word is worth."

She gestured to Macrae and Killigrew to heave open the hatchway leading to the passengers' quarters. "Ay, sir. That you shall."

THE REEK OF fear was strong below decks, and Meg wrinkled her nose.

The first passenger cabin she came to was locked, and she told the two pirates accompanying her to break it open. They did so with grins of anticipation, and Meg wondered if her own face bore the same expression. Her heart rate was increasing, and sweat trickled between her shoulder blades.

The door creaked open, and Meg found herself face to face with an elderly woman whose ample bosom threatened to spill over the top of her low-cut blue dress.

"Mercy!" The woman fell to her knees. "Mercy! Spare me, I beg you. Take what valuables you want, but spare me."

Something about her was familiar. Meg cast her mind back to her days as a servant. A friend of Thomas Digges? One of his many sisters, perhaps? No matter. Her gaze fell on the necklace adorning the woman's plump neck.

"Your life is spared. And I'll have these as payment." She reached for the string of pearls and gave it a sharp tug. The clasp broke and the necklace came free.

"My pearls!"

"No, madam. Mine." Meg tossed the necklace to Killigrew, who stuffed it inside the bucket-top of his boots.

Leaving the woman staring after her, eyes wide, she turned on her heel and set off to investigate the cabin next door. A snickering Macrae and Killigrew followed her, breaking down doors at her request, confiscating any valuables they came across, and there were many, for only the wealthy could afford passage from Jamaica back to England.

If was fortunate for Thomas Digges and his sons that they were not among the passengers. Her veneer of civility would likely crack wide open if she encountered the three again. One of his plantation managers was on board, though, tasked with ensuring the dowry reached England safely. She took great pleasure in informing him that it was now in the hands of the infamous Murdering Meg.

As she moved along the dark passageway, opening cabin after cabin, and there was still no sign of the person she sought, her mood began to darken. Perhaps her informant had been wrong. A cloud of depression was settling on her when the door of the last cabin—a cramped room, surely not fit for a plantation owner's genteel daughter—finally thudded open. Meg ducked her head to avoid the lintel and stepped inside.

A whirlwind of flailing fists hit her, and she raised her hands in self-defence. "'Strewth!" She grabbed hold of the slim wrists and forced them down. "Stop that! You'll have my eyes out."

It was difficult manoeuvring in such a confined space, but she managed to get behind her yelling attacker—a curvaceous young woman with long, fair hair. Meg had recognised Alice Digges at once and thought her heart would burst with happiness.

As she pinned Alice's arms to her sides, Macrae and Killigrew popped their heads round the door and looked a question. Meg jerked her head at them to leave. Killigrew wrinkled that beaky nose of his and withdrew. With a shrug Macrae followed him.

"Unhand me, you brute!" Alice gave an angry wriggle.

That beautiful face, that quick temper, that intoxicating, much missed scent of warm skin and fresh sweat. Meg tightened her arms and pressed her nose into the fair hair, ignoring the indignant squeal her action provoked. The fragrance brought back such sweet memories she could feel the prick of tears. Alice's puppy fat had disappeared, and fine lines had appeared around her eyes, but considering five years had passed, she had changed very little.

"My father will hunt you down like the dog you are. And when he catches you, you will swing from the nearest yardarm."

Meg suppressed a smile at the bloodthirsty threat. "Then I must take that risk. For I let go of you once, my dear, and I have no intention of doing so again."

Her words made Alice freeze for a long moment, then she twisted like an eel in her efforts to get a good look at her captor. Meg laughed and loosened her grip, and the next minute startled green eyes were locked on her face.

"Meg?" Alice's voice was shaky. "Is it really you?"

"Ay. I told you that I'd—Devil take it!" For Alice's eyes had rolled up in her head, and her body was as limp as a rag doll.

Meg resisted the urge to roll her own eyes and lifted the swooning young woman into her arms. She ducked her head and eased herself and her precious cargo out into the cramped passage, then headed for the *Kestrel*.

"Good God! That villain is kidnapping Alice," called someone. The cabin doorways filled with passengers, gaping at Meg in wide-eyed horror.

Kidnapping, indeed! thought Meg. Did they but know it, she was taking Alice back where she belonged.

"Put her down this instant, you rogue!" The elderly woman who had donated her pearls blocked her way.

In truth, Meg admired anyone who would defend Alice, but she took care not to reveal that fact. Instead, she pinned the woman in blue with a murderous glare. The results were instant. The woman quailed and stepped back, her face gone pale, one hand pressed to her heaving bosom. Meg brushed past her without a word.

Macrae and Killigrew were waiting for Meg up on deck. As she strode past them, they glanced at one another, raised their eyebrows, and followed her. And if they had any remark to make about the unconscious woman in their Captain's arms, they wisely kept it to themselves.

A KNOCK AT the cabin door proved to be George, the cabin boy.

"Chicken feathers, Captain." He held out his hand. "With Cook's compliments."

Meg accepted the feathers. "By Heaven, lad, but you took your time." His eyes tracked from her to the young woman lying supine on her bunk and back again. She grinned. The men must be agog for news of their eccentric Captain's latest jape. Well, they would have to wait. "Thankee, George. You may go."

With a last reluctant glance at the sleeping beauty, the boy exited and closed the door softly behind him.

The *Kestrel*, her hold full of plunder, was sailing back to Tortuga, leaving Captain Bracegirdle to make what repairs he could to the damaged *Bristol* and limp for the nearest port not under Spanish control. The other ship had got off lightly. Some pirates would have slaughtered everyone on board and sent the brigantine to the ocean bottom. Meanwhile the quartermaster was supervising the tallying of the booty, which he would in due course divide into equal shares, and the carpenter, tutting all the while and shaking his head, was examining the damage to the *Kestrel* and estimating the cost of repairs.

Meg eyed the feathers and reached for her flint. It was providential that Cook was planning to make chicken broth tonight. Surgeon Avery had examined Alice and pronounced her in no danger—she had merely swooned. He'd recommended a good whiff of *sal volatile*.

"Pirates do not carry smelling salts," Meg told him with some asperity.

He rolled his eyes. "Well then. Burned feathers will do at a pinch."

Feathers it was, then. She struck a spark and set them alight. Supporting Alice with one hand, she positioned the smouldering quills so the pungent smoke would curl up into her nostrils. A wrinkling of a pert nose and a low groan were her reward. Then eyelids fluttered open, and she found herself captured by familiar eyes at close quarters. Willingly, she fell into their depths, until a burning sensation dragged her back to her surroundings.

"What the Devil?" She dropped the feathers, which landed on her thighs and started to char her breeches. "Argh!" She leaped to her feet, brushed the smouldering feathers to the floor, and stamped on them until they were well and truly out.

"I thought it was a dream," murmured Alice, "but no dream woman would curse so." Meg sat back down and sucked singed fingers. A small hand reached out and touched her cheek, tentatively at first, then more firmly. "Oh yes! You're warm, soft . . . real." Alice's lower lip trembled, and tears sparkled against her pale eyelashes.

Meg grabbed the hand and kissed its palm. "Do not cry, my love. I promised I'd come back for you, and so I did." To her dismay, Alice snatched her hand away and sat up.

"'Twas five years ago!" Anger brought a flush of colour to the pale cheeks. "A tragic accident, father said. When you ran from him that night, you made for the stables. The horses were badly startled. They trampled you to death." She paused, her gaze turned inward. "He told me your corpse was too battered for me to see it. That he'd already buried you." She turned an accusing gaze on Meg. "But you were not dead. Whereas I, I thought I would die of weeping for you."

Meg bit her lip. So that was Digges' story. Eventually she would have to tell Alice the truth—when she saw Meg's scarred back, she was bound to ask. It would break her heart to hear how the menfolk in her family had behaved.

"I beg your pardon," she said. "I would not have hurt you for the world." Alice's gaze remained unforgiving. "Truly," pleaded Meg, "I did come close to death."

Thomas's vicious whipping of her should have been punishment enough, but Dudley and Titus had happened on the scene and learned what had provoked it. That an indentured servant—a woman no less!—should be discovered in their sister's bed . . . They had resolved to teach her the error of her unnatural ways.

"But you were not dead," repeated Alice, her voice hard. In Meg's dreams, Alice had always taken her back with an eager and loving smile.

"No. But for a long time I did not know who I was."

She remembered Thomas Digges' shocked expression when he had found her later that night, her life hanging by a thread. Even *he* had not thought his sons would go so far. True, she was little better than a slave, but she was white and a woman too. Throwing her body into the sea must have seemed the only way to avoid bringing more shame on his family. But she had survived.

A hand grabbed her forearm, closing unknowingly on her recent cut, and she tried not to flinch.

"Is that why you did not come for me?" Alice's voice was outraged. "You had forgot me?"

Meg wondered if she should go down on her knees and beg for forgiveness. She gave a sheepish nod. "In the beginning at least."

She had regained consciousness on board a fishing smack, snagged by the fishermen's nets. They had thought her dead; certainly her body was so torn and bruised they feared at first she would not live. But their womenfolk, with their chapped hands and kind hearts, had nursed her back to health. She made sure to repay their kindness with booty from her first successful raid.

"Later . . . well." Meg willed Alice to understand. "I knew that to keep my promise I must take you back by force. But an attack on your father's plantation was beyond my reach." She raised her hands and let them fall. "It took me longer than expected to get my own crew, my own brigantine . . ."

"Longer than expected? Five *years*, Meg!" Alice looked distressed. "He was sending me to England."

Ah. Meg's anxiety eased. This was surely the true source of Alice's anger. "To marry his business partner. I know. When I learned of it, I vowed to prevent it, whatever the cost."

At last Alice's gaze softened.

A belated thought struck Meg and set her heart pounding. "I . . . Did you want to marry him?"

Alice smiled and relaxed back against the pillows. "No," she said quietly, "I had no wish to become Mrs. John Bellamy. After your death, I resigned myself to my fate. But now you have returned to me."

She reached for Meg's hand and squeezed it, and any awkwardness remaining dissipated as they contented themselves with gazing into each other's eyes.

After a while, Alice turned her attention to her surroundings, her gaze darting round the cabin before returning to Meg. "Am I aboard your ship?"

Meg nodded. "The *Kestrel*."

That got her a wide-eyed look. "You're Murdering Meg?"

She stood and made Alice a courtly bow. "At your service, milady."

"Those terrible tales are true?"

Meg gave her a crooked smile. "Perhaps."

Alice's eyes widened even further. "The bloodlust, the cruelty?"

"Only if Cook burns my breakfast."

"The ravaging of women?"

"That tale is true indeed. Oof!" Alice's hand had slapped Meg in the belly. "No," she amended. "Though several wenches have offered to pay me a pretty penny for my services." She winked.

"I'll wager!"

They chuckled over that for a while, then Alice raised a hand to her mouth. "By Heaven, but my father will have palpitations when he hears that Murdering Meg has carried off his only daughter!"

Meg's lips thinned. "Indeed I hope so."

It was fortunate that a knock at the cabin door diverted the questioning her response provoked. The quartermaster peeked round it, nodded politely at Alice, and turned his attention to Meg.

"The division of the spoils is complete, Captain. 'Tis a good haul, more than expected. There'll be celebrations tonight."

"Thankee, Mr. Mostyn. But you may put my portion back into the pot."

His eyebrows rose. "Do you not want your usual share-and-a-quarter?"

"I have all the treasure I want right here." She glanced at Alice and enjoyed the rosy blush that covered her cheeks.

"As you wish. I'll tell the men the good news." Mostyn turned to go.

"Tell them 'tis only this one time, mind," she called after him. "Next time, the division will be as usual."

"Ay, Captain."

"Oh, and break out the bumbo." Her men were partial to the concoction of rum, water, sugar, and nutmeg. "We'll drink a toast to our dead shipmates."

"Ay, ay, Captain." The door thudded closed behind him.

"Did you mean that?" asked Alice, her gaze serious. "About the treasure?"

"Alice." Meg moved closer and slipped an arm round her waist. "With all my heart I meant it. Only the thought of being with you has kept me from losing my wits all these years." She leaned over and placed a kiss on a soft cheek. "I've a house in Tortuga, a fine home it is too, with servants well paid and loyal to me. But 'tis lonely there for all that. Come live with me. Let us pick up where we left off."

Alice gave her an enigmatic smile. "Could any lady resist such an invitation from a pirate?"

Meg squeezed her. "Do not keep me in suspense, wench. What is your answer?"

The smile widened. "Why, I accept, Captain Etherege. What other answer could there be?"

Alice wound her hands behind Meg's neck and pulled her close. They kissed, tentatively at first, then more deeply, reconnecting after five long years of loneliness and at times despair.

At last, a need to breathe made them break the kiss. "'Twas so long ago, can you truly remember where we left off?" murmured Alice, her colour heightened.

Meg kicked off her boots, tore off her doublet, shirt, and breeches, and climbed onto the bunk beside her. "Ay, that I can."

So impatient was Meg to rid her prize of dress, bodice, and chemise, she tore buttons, laces, and fabric in her haste. Alice protested at such harsh treatment of her clothing, but Meg's, "I shall buy you new ones when we get ashore, my sweet," soon stifled her half-hearted objections.

The final garment came loose, and with a glad cry Meg flung it across the cabin and turned to regard pearls more valuable than any among her plunder. She caressed a creamy breast with one hand and bent her head to the other.

Alice trembled at her touch and moaned in a most gratifying manner. Meg continued her attentions for a while longer, then raised her head. "The question is, can you?"

"Can I what?" Alice's face was the picture of confusion and frustration.

"Why, remember what we were about when your father caught us."

"'Tis burned into my brain, love." Alice pulled her close once more. "My fervent hope," she whispered in Meg's ear, "is that *this time* matters will be allowed to proceed to a satisfactory conclusion!"

"'Tis my hope too," said Meg. And willingly she applied herself to the task.

2

PLANTER'S PUNCH

HEADS TURNED IN Meg's direction, and the conversation died as she lurched through the door into the smoke-wreathed bar of The Catt and Fiddle. Eyes widened as the regulars took in her battered appearance and bloody shirt.

"Best not let Murdering Meg catch you staring," muttered someone. "She'll have your eyes out, and that's on a good day."

The heads quickly turned away again.

"Over here, Captain," came Mostyn's voice from the corner. The *Kestrel*'s grizzled quartermaster was sitting at a table with Coke and two of her crewmen.

She raised a hand to acknowledge his hail and weaved between the tables and chairs towards him.

As she pulled out a stool and sat, the gaunt sailing master pushed the jug of rum punch towards her. "Look like you could use some of this, Captain."

"Thankee but no, Mr. Coke." She shook her head and instantly regretted it as the throbbing intensified. "I have not the stomach for Kill-Devil." She focussed on not being sick. Not that there could be much left to throw up; she had puked up her guts twice already on the run from her house to the harbour-front tavern.

"Your head's bleeding!" Mostyn frowned.

Meg touched a hand to her temple and examined it. The bleeding had almost stopped. "Looks worse than 'tis."

"What happened?"

"Cut throats, four of them. Must have known it was the maid's day off. They stove in my front door and tried to stave in my skull too." She was lucky they had been content to use cudgels rather than cutlasses. "They took Mistress Digges." She kept her voice steady with an effort

The younger and beakier-nosed of the two sailors leaned forward. "She could still be in hiding—"

"What kind of fool d'ye take me for, Killigrew?" snarled Meg. "Think you I did not tear the house apart searching for her?"

When she had awoken on the floor of her drawing room, her head splitting, she had known at once that Alice was gone—the quality of the silence, perhaps. But she had checked the kitchen and upstairs chambers anyway. As she had feared, no Alice emerged from the shadows, smiling in the way that made Meg's heart sing.

Killigrew reddened and sat back. An uneasy silence fell, then Coke cleared his throat and ventured, "But what can they want with her, Captain?"

The memory of Alice's face, cheeks ashen, eyes wide with fear, made Meg's stomach churn. "'Tis surely someone's attempt to even the score with me."

The other sailor, Macrae, gave her a nervous glance and gulped his rum before speaking. "No Tortuga man would harm a fellow Brethren of the Coast, Captain."

The quartermaster shook his head. "If the rewards were high enough he might."

"And risk word getting back, Mr. Mostyn?" Macrae's thick eyebrows rose. "'Tis too small an island for news of such treachery not to spread and fast."

"Ay," said Meg thoughtfully. "Which means the rogues are outsiders."

Killigrew licked his lips. "Could it be the Dutchman?"

She gave him a sharp look. "What makes you think 'tis him, sir?"

That "sir" encouraged him. "The *Evening Star* was moored here earlier. She weighed anchor two hours ago."

The *Evening Star* was Pieter Hendricksz's brigantine. And Hendricksz's base was Port Royal not Tortuga. The timing was right too. Meg frowned. "But why would the Dutchman—?"

"His men were in here earlier," broke in Mostyn. "I heard them talking. A Jamaican sugar planter has promised them a hefty sum. What the nature of their commission is, though—" He shrugged.

A revelation left Meg feeling winded. "For the love of God!"

"Captain?"

All eyes were on her.

"'Tis Thomas Digges, lads. It must be." She sighed. "He's paid to get his daughter back."

"OW!" SAID MEG. "Hold that lantern closer, Killigrew, so the Surgeon can see what he's doing."

The sailor obliged but it made little difference.

"'S blood, but that bodkin of yours is blunt, Mr. Avery!"

"Nearly done, Captain. Another stitch. There." He bit off the thread and stood back to admire his handiwork. Then he patted her on the shoulder. "'Tis lucky you have so rock hard a skull. That blow should have killed you." He busied himself stowing needle and twine in his surgeon's chest.

She grunted and glanced up at the bellying topsails then astern to where the turtle-backed silhouette that was Tortuga was receding into the distance. Coke was at the helm and he had set the *Kestrel*'s course west southwest, hugging the coast of Hispaniola before leaving the shelter of coastal waters and venturing out into the Windward Passage. At this time of year, the trade winds would sweep them to Jamaica at top speed, but that wouldn't help much.

"The *Evening Star* has half a day's head start." Meg thumped her fist on the rail. "God rot Hendricksz! If he so much as touches a hair on her head . . ."

"Digges will have stipulated she must be returned unharmed," soothed Mostyn, who had come up beside her.

She should have known the old man wouldn't take the theft of his daughter and her dowry lying down. Alice's hand was meant to seal the contract between Digges and a business partner, but Meg and Alice had had other ideas. Now she could kick herself. She had felt safe on Tortuga, let down her guard. And it was Alice who was paying the price.

Sailors busied themselves all about her, manning the *Kestrel*'s ropes or scrambling up the rigging barefoot. She had expected problems mustering a skeleton crew at such short notice, for the gist of the *Kestrel*'s articles was clear: "No prey, no pay" and the coins were meagre and coming from her own pocket. But to her relief more than enough men had volunteered. Indeed some seemed only too eager to escape wives and whores that had apparently started nagging them after a mere week in port.

Familiarity breeds contempt indeed, thought Meg with wry amusement.

The quartermaster and sailing master had everything under control, so there was nothing for her to do except twiddle her thumbs for a day and a half while the *Kestrel* covered the three hundred miles to Port Royal. Which was a mixed blessing, as keeping busy would have helped to keep her from dwelling on Alice's plight.

With an irritated shake of the head she pushed aside the disquieting thoughts that had been her constant companion since she discovered Alice was gone.

Maybe sleep would help ease this pounding in my skull. "I'll be in my cabin, Mr. Mostyn."

"Ay, Captain," he said. "Sleep well."

NO SOUND CAME from the quarter boat except the muffled swish of oars as it made its way between other vessels, at this hour little more than silhouettes with riding lights hanging from their rigging. Ahead, in the deeper section of the harbour, the brigantine that was their quarry bobbed at anchor. As they drew closer, Meg skinned both eyes and ears, but there was no sign of activity on board the *Evening Star*.

The fox and his chicken have flown the coop.

She must make sure before she went haring off to Digges' sugar plantation, though. There was a faint possibility another planter was behind Alice's abduction, though what his motive could be the Lord alone knew. And, she conceded with an internal wince, she'd rather not go back to the Digges estate if she could avoid it. To say it held bad memories was something of an understatement.

"Steady, lads," she whispered, as they closed on their target. "A little more to port. That's it. Rest your oars."

They came to a stop alongside the brigantine's hull with barely a whisper. Meg held her breath and listened but heard only the slap of water, the creak of rigging, and distant, raucous voices carrying across the harbour. At this time of night Port Royal's streets and alleyways were packed with those seeking entertainment at the taverns and brothels springing up everywhere.

"Killigrew, Macrae," she murmured. "With me. The rest of you stay here."

Meg reached for the grappling iron and stood up, compensating by instinct as the boat rocked under her. She let fly, and a second later heard the barbs thud home. A tug on the rope satisfied her it was secure. After checking that her loaded flintlock was tucked safely in her belt, she took a firm grasp on the rope and hauled herself up it, hand over hand. It was hard work that made her head ache even more, and she was soon breathless.

Before peering over the rail, she paused and listened for signs of activity. Was that the faint slap of cards on the deck and the murmur of men's voices? *The night watch. Preoccupied, by the sound of it.* Which meant she should be able to slip on board without discovery and explore her surroundings.

Moments later the silent shapes that were Killigrew and Macrae joined her, and she pointed to the open hatchway from which the voices were coming. She mimed instructions and received nods of comprehension in return. When they were in position she drew her cutlass and stepped boldly through the hatchway door.

"Well, well. What have we here?"

The three men playing cards in the lantern light looked as if they'd seen a ghost. One let out an oath, grabbed for his cutlass, and sprang to his feet.

"Steady," warned Meg.

Her men emerged from the shadows, pistols cocked. The card players froze.

"Murdering Meg, at your service." She gave them a mock bow, lifting her head in time to see the exchange of panicked glances. "You've heard of me? Good. Now. I'll wager you know already that your Captain has taken something that belongs to me. Something precious." She scowled, and they took a nervous step back. "So we can do this easy or hard. Hard involves skinning you alive." She brandished her cutlass, and heard audible swallows. "Which is it to be, lads?"

"Easy?" suggested the plump man with the plaited beard.

"A man of good sense. Excellent. Then answer me this. Where is the Dutchman, and where is the young woman he stole from me?"

"Ashore," he answered at once. His companions nodded.

"Together?"

"Ay." He glanced at the others. "He's taking her to some sugar plantation that lies between Port Royal and the Blue Mountains."

"Thomas Digges' place?" The location sounded right.

He shrugged. "Never heard the name."

"Nor I," said the skinny man with the scar on his temple. "'Tis the woman's father, though. That much I know."

Meg sighed. It looked as if she'd have to face her unpleasant memories after all. "How long ago did they go ashore?"

The three men looked at one another, then the grubby one with the eye patch who had remained silent until now said, "Five hours ago, mayhap?"

His friends nodded. "Ay. About that."

"Plague take him! Oh, don't look so worried, lads. I may not like your answer, but I won't kill you for it." She nodded to Macrae and Killigrew. "Our business is concluded. Back to the quarter boat."

"Ay, Captain," they chorused.

MEG ELBOWED HER way up the street, ignoring the oaths and exclamations that followed her. The quarter boat was on its way back to the *Kestrel*, having dropped Meg and her two companions ashore. Mostyn was in command of the ship now, with orders to give her two days before coming after her. If she wasn't back by then, something had gone seriously awry.

"Where are we bound, Captain?" asked Macrae, as they hurried past a gunsmith's, an ivory turner's shop, and a door bearing a chirurgeon's brass plate.

"There's a livery stable here somewhere. We need horses," she explained. "'Tis a goodly ride to Digges' estate."

His thick eyebrows drew together at the prospect. "You know it?"

"Ay," she muttered. "For my sins."

The livery stable when they found it was closed and no amount of shouting or battering on the doors could rouse the lad in charge. Meg used her cutlass to force open a window, slipped inside, and unbolted the doors. They found the stable lad curled up on a heap of fresh hay, snoring loudly and smelling of rum. Killigrew tried to wake him but failed. Meg rolled her eyes, dropped a handful of *reales* on the boy's chest, and set about selecting and saddling a horse. Her two crewmen did likewise. Around them the stable's occupants snorted, huffed, and moved restlessly in their stalls.

At last, the horse tacked to her satisfaction, Meg put her booted foot in the stirrup and mounted up. Outside, she waited, soothing her mount and trying to still her impatience, for Macrae and Killigrew to join her. When they did so she beckoned.

"With me, lads," she called, and dug in her heels.

DAWN WAS BREAKING, the bats flittering back to their roosts, the dawn chorus of parrots, finches, and parakeets well underway, when they emerged from the forest that bordered the Digges estate. Meg reined her mount to a halt and gave the cloud-covered tops of the Blue Mountains to the northeast a wistful glance. She had removed her doublet, but her shirt and breeches were sticking to her, and she was missing a stiff sea breeze. Macrae and Killigrew didn't look much better. They were red faced and, from their constant shifting about, saddle sore.

A pineapple plant stood close by. Meg cut off the ripest looking of the fruits with her cutlass, sliced off the ridged skin, and bit into the tart, juicy flesh. When she'd quenched hunger and thirst, she handed what was left to Macrae and Killigrew and wiped her sticky fingers on her breeches.

Blocking out the sounds of their slurping and chewing, she pondered which way to go. It would be best to avoid the manager's house, the workshops, and the street of shacks where the slaves and indentured servants lived—not that many were likely to recognise her as the young white woman who had vanished in such mysterious circumstances five-and-a-half years ago. But at this time of day, the sugar works should be deserted.

"This way." She turned the horse west onto a rutted track that skirted an area of recently harvested sugar cane. Macrae and Killigrew threw away what was left of their pineapple and followed.

As she rode, memories mobbed her like unwelcoming ghosts. When the sugar works came into sight she broke into even more of a sweat. The mill's massive iron rollers, powered by two oxen, had crushed a man's arm once, she remembered with a shudder; their incessant rumble still sometimes invaded her dreams. As she rode past the boiling sheds, she remembered the stinking heat of the interior, where workers scooped scum off the cane juice that kept seething in the great kettles. And yet, if she hadn't come to this hellhole she would never have met the planter's pretty young daughter and found to her delight that her feelings were reciprocated.

I'll get Alice back if 'tis the last thing I do.

"Where do they make the rum?" asked Killigrew, looking around. She pointed to the still house. He sniffed and looked unimpressed.

They left the sugar works behind and rode past fields of cane awaiting harvesting, then started up the hill that overlooked the plantation. Its lower slopes were densely wooded.

As they wound their way between the tree trunks, Meg caught glimpses of the great house that was her destination. Alice's father had spent a small fortune carting in the seasoned timber needed to build it—nothing but the best for the Digges family. He'd made several changes to the house and its environs, she saw. The copse of *lignum vitae* to the east had gone, for a start. She used to hide there, waiting for Alice to sneak down from her bedchamber—they had shared their first kiss there among the lavender-coloured blossoms.

The sky was growing lighter by the minute, and smoke curled up from one of the chimneys. The servants must be up and about, getting the house and its inhabitants ready to face another day.

As they'd seen no sign of the Dutchman on the way here, she presumed he had stayed overnight, enjoying Digges' hospitality. She rested her hand on the hilt of her cutlass and imagined slitting his throat, then reined her horse to a halt and dismounted.

Macrae and Killigrew halted too and looked down at her.

"On foot from here on, lads."

"Ay, Captain." They dismounted, clearly glad to give their aching backsides a rest.

Leaving the horses tethered to a branch, they slunk towards the servants' entrance, taking advantage of the natural cover when they could, sprinting when they couldn't. At last they reached the back door.

Macrae drew his pistol, but Meg shook her head and put a finger to her lips. He shoved the flintlock back in his belt and drew his cutlass instead.

Drawing her own cutlass, she eased through the door into the kitchen. A pretty young maid gasped at her entrance and took a step back. From the empty jugs lined up on the table and the kettle of water hanging over the roaring hearth, she was heating water for the morning wash.

"Steady now," soothed Meg, giving the girl her most charming smile. "I won't harm you. My business is with the master of the house."

"Is it indeed?" The maid jumped as Macrae and Killigrew appeared.

"Leave your work and sit over there." Meg indicated a chair, and after a moment the girl took it.

As Meg sheathed her cutlass and told her men to do the same, the tension in the room eased. She returned her attention to the maid.

"What's your name?"

"Annie Chapman. What's yours?"

The spirited reply made Meg's lips quirk. "Margaret Etherege. But you may call me Meg." There was no recognition in those dark eyes, but then the girl had obviously taken up her position with the Digges household after Meg left. "Tell me, Mistress Chapman," she continued, "did your master have any visitors last night?"

The maid cocked her head while she considered, then gave a nod.

"Was one of them his daughter?"

She gave another nod.

"Ah." Meg didn't care whether her relief was obvious. "And where is Mistress Digges now?"

"Locked in her bed chamber."

He's taking no risks. "Is it still at the back? On the second floor? By the privy?"

The maid blinked at Meg. "Yes. But how—?"

"The man who brought her here, the buccaneer. Was he alone?"

"He had a man with him. Shared a bedchamber last night, they did. Servants' quarters should've been good enough for the likes of them but—" She sniffed her disdain, glanced at the kitchen clock, and frowned. "The master'll be wanting his hot water."

"Let him wait."

Footsteps were approaching along the passageway, and Meg signalled to Macrae and Killigrew. They pressed their backs to the wall and waited, cutlasses at the ready.

An old man in butler's garb stepped through the open door. He stopped at the sight of Meg, his face going ashen. "Good God!" Then Macrae and Killigrew stepped into view, and he went even paler.

"And a good day to you too, Mr. Phillips," said Meg. "Come in, come in." She beckoned. Reluctantly he shuffled further into the kitchen, and Macrae pushed the door closed behind him.

Meg saw the butler glance at Annie. "Unharmed, as you see, sir. Only those who stand in my way will get hurt. I've come for Mistress Digges."

"I *knew* Digges should not have done it," he muttered. "Dragging her back here against her will. But he would have his daughter, come Hell or high water."

"Hell, undoubtedly," said Meg grimly, "if he won't return her to me."

He threw her an exasperated glance. "You know he will not. You hit him where it hurts, Mistress Etherege. In his pride."

"His pocket, more like. And if anyone deserved it, it was Thomas Digges. Not to mention those fine, upstanding sons of his. How stands the tally of those women they have got bastards on these days?"

Phillips winced. " 'Tis true they have no manners and no scruples."

"Like father, like son."

He gave her an owlish look. "You're a fine one to talk of scruples! Stealing his daughter and her dowry—"

"Oh!" Annie's eyes widened. "You're *that* Meg."

Meg ignored her. "Think you Mistress Digges was unwilling when I took her from the *Bristol*, sir? I swear to you she was not. She viewed it as rescue from an unwelcome marriage."

"I—"

"Ask her, if you doubt me. She was exceeding unwilling to go with the Dutchman, however. Oh. Did I not mention him? His men broke into our house on Tortuga, kidnapped her, and near cudgelled my brains out. And now, sir, he is your master's honoured guest." Recounting recent events had made her angry, and she took a moment to regain her composure. "Digges loves his daughter only for the money and influence she can bring him."

Phillips raised his hands and let them fall. "But what can *I* do?"

"Help me get her back."

He shook his head. "My allegiance must be to my master."

Meg glared at him but saw he would not budge. But he was an honourable man, in his way, and she would not harm him for it. "As you wish. But stay out of my way." The butler gave her a slow, grudging nod. It would have to do.

She turned to Macrae and Killigrew. "Keep an eye on these two. I'm going to get Mistress Digges." The route to Alice's bedroom was branded into Meg's memory.

"What if someone should see you and raise the alarm?" asked Macrae.

"Digges and his sons are still abed. As for the servants, I'll take my chances—I doubt they will intervene."

"But—"

She cut him off with a slicing gesture. "Enough. There is no more time to be lost. If you hear a commotion, come to my aid."

Killigrew elbowed his shipmate into silence. "Ay, Captain, we will," he said. "Good luck."

MEG COULD HEAR the sobs even through the thickness of the door. She balled her hands into fists. *They'll pay for making Alice weep.*

The key was missing, so she drew her cutlass and set to work, digging the sharp edge into the area around the lock. Inside the bedchamber the sobs faltered then stopped, and she sensed its occupant listening intently. Wood chips and splinters showered the toes of her boots as she dug and hacked, until at last the door gave. With an impatient grunt she hurled her full weight against it and lurched through.

"Meg!" Alice flew at her. She was wearing an unflattering nightgown, and her eyes were red with crying, but to Meg she had never looked more beautiful. "I thought you were dead!" cried Alice, clinging to her as though she meant never to let her go again. "Your head was bleeding so." She seemed torn between smiling and bursting into yet more tears.

"Shh! You'll wake the household." Meg stroked Alice's hair. "It takes more than a cudgel to put Murdering Meg out of action, my dear." She kissed Alice soundly then gave her a grin.

Alice smiled at her in return, but her smile faltered. "We must leave here at once, Meg. Before my father learns of your presence."

"Ay. Come, my—"

"You told me she was dead!" came an angry bellow from the landing.

"Devil take it!" muttered Meg, as Thomas Digges appeared in the doorway. The planter's grey hair was in disarray and his nightgown bulged over a belly even more prominent than the one she remembered.

"My men led me to believe her dead," said his companion, moving into view. He was a strikingly handsome man, as tall as Digges was short, with flowing brown hair and a neat moustache in the latest style. Muscled shoulders and biceps filled out his doublet and shirt, and a cutlass hung at his belt. "Did you not, Cawthorne?"

"We thought she was, Captain," came a man's voice from the landing.

"You must be the Dutchman," said Meg. "Margaret Etherege, at your service. My apologies for not being dead."

"None necessary, madam. 'Tis easily remedied." Hendricksz grinned at her, a gold front tooth winking.

Meg sheltered Alice with her body and raised her cutlass. "Step aside and let us through, gentlemen."

"Damned if I will!" said Digges.

"Damned if you won't." She took a step towards him, and he flinched and scuttled out of sight.

Meg arched an eyebrow at the man who remained. "'Tis not your fight, Dutchman. Let us pass, and I'll think no more of your part in this affair."

Hendricksz considered then gave a nod. "As you wish."

"Not so fast, sir," came Thomas Digges' indignant voice. "I paid you to kill this she devil." His words made Alice suck in her breath. "Do it, or I'll have my coin back."

The Dutchman's eyes flashed. "Have a care." He turned his head, the better to address the plantation owner. "No one speaks to me so and lives to tell the tale."

There was a moment's tense silence. "I meant no disrespect," said Digges. "But you can understand the source of my dissatisfaction, surely? For the terms of our agreement specified . . ." He trailed off.

Hendricksz rubbed his jaw. "'Tis true that one particular clause remains unfulfilled." His head snapped round to face Meg once more. "Alas, I have no choice." He made her a mock bow. "My apologies, Mistress Etherege, but I have my reputation to consider."

He drew his cutlass, and as he did so Alice cried out, "Meg!"

"Fear not, my dear. For the Dutchman has his reputation, but so do I." Meg cocked her pistol and pressed it into Alice's shaking hands. "Take this."

"But—"

"Stand clear." She urged Alice to one side.

The grinning buccaneer stepped into the bedchamber and closed with Meg at once. That first encounter nearly cost her dearly. His reach was longer than hers, his strength greater, so that parrying his blade left her feeling both bruised and winded. After a little while, though, by mutual consent, they paused to recover their breath. She glanced at her bleeding right wrist—it was sheer luck he hadn't sliced through the tendon, or worse—then at him.

"You're no match for me." He gave her a wolfish smile.

"We'll see about that!" Sparks flew as they engaged once more.

Up and down Alice's bedchamber they fought, lunging and grappling, slashing and hacking, jumping from floor to bed to dresser to floor again. Costly bedlinen tore under boot heels, candlesticks and precious ornaments went flying, and cuts and gouges marred furniture shipped all the way from England at huge expense.

Hendricksz managed a glancing slash across Meg's right biceps. She clapped her hand to the stinging cut and examined the blood on her palm. The wound wasn't deep. It annoyed her more to see the mess his blade was making of the shirt Alice had sewed for her.

The fight continued. Several times Meg tried to get behind him, but each time she failed. Then a moment's inattention saw her catch her heel in the bed linen and lose her balance. With a triumphant roar the Dutchman threw himself at her, but before his cutlass could strike the fatal blow a chamber pot—empty, fortunately—sailed out of nowhere, struck his sword arm, and smashed into the wall.

"Why, you—" Enraged that the distraction had enabled Meg to escape, he turned, and slashed at Alice, who shrieked and only just evaded the razor edge in time.

"Coward!" cried a horrified Meg. "Dog!" Then, to Alice. "To the door, my dear, and quickly." Now Alice had abandoned her neutrality, Hendricksz would see her as fair game.

When Meg glanced round to see why Alice hesitated, she saw a nightgown-clad figure blocking the doorway, watching the fight with his arms folded over his fat stomach and a smirk on his face. An instant later, two familiar figures appeared on either side of Digges: his sons, Dudley and Titus.

Meg's stomach churned, as she remembered the last time they had met. *Devil take them!*

"Meg, beware!"

Alice's shriek cut through Meg's paralysis. Instinct made her duck and roll, and the Dutchman's blade slashed through the space her neck had occupied an instant earlier. The hairs on the nape of her neck stood up at her narrow escape.

"'S blood, but you have the luck of the Devil!" he cried.

Meg bared her teeth. "And a miss is as good as a mile." She glanced to where Alice had taken refuge in a corner. "The pistol, Alice. If he goes for you again—"

Alice gave the heavy flintlock a doubtful glance. "I don't think I can."

"Just aim and pull the trigger!"

Meg glanced towards the door again then blinked in pleased astonishment. Digges and his sons had vanished, replaced by Macrae and Killigrew, who were leaning against the doorjamb, wearing relaxed grins.

"All shipshape, Captain," called Macrae, giving her the thumbs up. He brandished his flintlock at Hendricksz. "Shall I—?"

She shook her head. "We'll fight this one fair, but you may protect Mistress Digges. Alice." She gestured the younger woman towards the door. "Take cover." Keeping one eye on the Dutchman, Alice scurried to safety.

Now all Meg had to do was worry about herself. She turned to face her opponent, who was breathing hard and sweating as much as she was. "I grow weary of this," she called. "Let's finish it."

Hendricksz grinned, but this time there was no humour in it. "My pleasure."

He raised his cutlass and rushed her. For a moment they strained to and fro, then Meg pretended to give way and, in that instant when he was off balance, ducked under his guard, straightened, and brought her knee up, hard.

"Agh!"

Any normal man would have clasped both hands round his stones, but Hendricksz was made of sterner stuff. Though his expression was pained and he faltered, he brought his cutlass round in a sweeping cut that would have severed her backbone . . . had she still been there. But that momentary distraction had given her the opening she needed, and she took full advantage of it to get behind him, giving his left thigh a vicious slash in the process.

Flesh parted under her blade before bone jarred the cutlass to a halt, then came the hot gush of blood over her hand. Hendricksz cried out in pain, dropped his cutlass, and twisted round, clapping his hand to the wounded thigh, from which bright red blood was already pumping. But it was too late, and as they locked gazes, she could see that he knew.

"You have done for me!" His tone was one of disbelief.

"Ay," said Meg.

The Dutchman lifted a hand to his forehead, leaving a bloody smear. Then he staggered and dropped to his right knee, before crumpling forward onto his face.

For a few seconds there was no sound in the bedchamber except Meg's panting and, incongruously, a bird singing just outside the window. She wiped her cutlass on the back of his doublet, and cast an exhausted glance towards the door. Alice was hurrying towards her, arms outstretched.

"Hold." Meg held up a gory hand in warning. "You'll spoil your nightgown."

"Think you I care about that?" Alice took her in her arms, and for a long moment they let their embraces and eyes speak for them. Then Meg took Alice's hand and led her to the door.

On the landing outside the bedchamber, a satisfying sight met her eyes. Digges and his two sons were kneeling on the polished floorboards, hands bound behind them. Macrae and Killigrew smirked at her.

"Well done, lads." She pursed her lips. "Where's the other one? The Dutchman's man, Cawthorne?"

"Said it was his Captain's fight. Ran for it." Killigrew rubbed his jaw and grinned.

Meg chuckled.

"Your wounds need tending, Meg," interrupted Alice. "Annie."

Only then did Meg notice the huddle of servants gathered at the top of the stairs, watching events. At Alice's hail, the maid started along the landing towards them. Meg shook her head, and Annie Chapman halted in confusion.

"In a minute," explained Meg. "I have business to attend to."

One at a time she hauled Digges and his sons to their feet. They were trembling and couldn't seem to take their eyes off her bloody shirt. Before she could address them, however, Alice elbowed her aside and reached for her father's fat neck.

"How could you pay someone to kill Meg?" she bellowed, hands squeezing, face the very picture of fury. "I hate you. I hate you. I hate you!"

"Alice!" Meg prised Alice's fingers from his throat.

"But—" For a moment Alice resisted her then all the fight went out of her.

"No, I prithee." Meg led Alice away from her father, who looked as taken aback by his daughter's transformation into an avenging fury as Meg felt. "Do not stoop to your father's level."

"He is no father of mine." Alice turned to glare at her brothers. "Nor are you any longer my kin."

The brothers exchanged a sullen glance and the older and fatter one, Titus, shrugged. "Why should we care?"

His tone offended Meg. She pretended to take the question seriously. "Think on this, sir. Your sister's renunciation puts me in something of a quandary. For I had resolved not to kill any member of her family in front of her. But as you no longer *are* a member of her family . . ."

At the implication, Titus went so pale she thought he was going to swoon.

She curled her lip. "Fear not. I am grown weary of bloodletting."

Alice drew her aside. "Did I hear you right?" she asked, her voice low. "You mean to let them live?"

Meg was glad to see that the angry flush had faded, and Alice seemed more composed. "Ay."

"But—after all the injury they have done you?"

"They deserve to die, 'tis true." Meg cupped Alice's cheek and stroked her thumb across it. "But, much as I would like to kill them, I fear I cannot. For even though you have denied them, they are still your kin, my love. And in time memories of such a bloody deed might come between us."

"Never!" declared Alice.

Meg took her hand and pressed it. "Call me a coward, but I will not risk it."

Alice sighed but her frown smoothed. "You are no coward," she murmured.

Killigrew had overheard their whispered conversation and he fingered the hilt of his cutlass. "I could finish 'em off for you, Captain. Would that not kill two birds with one stone?"

"A generous offer indeed, Killigrew. But I cannot accept. Unlike Mr. Digges," she fixed the planter with a glare and raised her voice, "I do my own killing."

Hatred filled Digges' gaze. "Murdering whore! I rue the day my family set eyes on you."

"Strangely, I do not. But then, that was the day I met your daughter." She smiled. "As for calling me a murderer? Was it not rather *you* who tried to kill *me*? And thrice at that?"

So fast, the plantation owner had no time even to blink, she drew back her fist and punched him in the face. He staggered and would have fallen had not Macrae steadied him. Beside her, Alice began to laugh.

Meg shook her stinging hand and regarded with a sense of satisfaction the damage she had wrought. Digges' lip was split, and his nose broken. It was worth the minor discomfort of bruised knuckles.

" 'Twould be but natural justice to take your life," she continued, her voice hard as granite. "But for your daughter's sake, I have decided to be merciful. As for your sons . . ." She gathered the saliva in her mouth and spat at them in turn. As her spittle ran down their cheeks, and they screwed up their faces in disgust, she leaned closer and lowered her voice. " 'Tis not pleasant to be treated with such contempt, is it, by God? But 'tis little enough considering what you did to me." She put her finger to her lips as if considering. "Too little, mayhap. Shall I thrust my sword hilt up your arses?" The brothers blenched. "Or cut off your manhoods?" Dudley let out a strangled moan. For a moment longer, Meg kept the two in suspense, then she stepped back. Their shoulders sagged with relief.

"Listen well," she said, holding each prisoner's gaze in turn. "If I ever see your faces again, I will not be so merciful." She raised her voice to a bellow. "I will hang, draw, and quarter you. You have my word on it."

Someone took her hand and pressed the bruised knuckles to soft lips. It was Alice, and she was smiling.

"Come, my dear," said Meg. "I need my wounds tended, and, more importantly, a clean shirt. And you cannot leave here in your night dress." Alice nodded and signalled Annie to approach. "After that, we must be on our way. For 'tis a long ride back to Port Royal.

"In the mean time," she continued, turning to address Killigrew and Macrae, "search the house, and if you spy aught of value belonging to its owners—not the servants, mind—help yourselves and use my horse to transport it back to the *Kestrel*. For of a certainty," she glanced at Digges and his sons, "they are hardly in a position to object."

MEG HELD ALICE close, nibbled a delicate ear, and breathed into it, "I'm never letting you out of my arms again."

A flock of green parakeets burst out of the forest on their right, calling loudly, and Alice followed their flight before twisting in the saddle to look at Meg. "Even so, we should have ridden separately. This poor horse!"

Meg gave the mount they had liberated from Digges' stable an amused glance. It was a strapping animal, well fed and in good condition, and no doubt accustomed to carrying much heavier cargo in the form of fat planters or sacks of sugar. "Spare it your pity, my sweet. For how could it wish to be anywhere other than between your thighs?"

Alice's cheeks flushed a pretty shade of pink. "Sauce!" But she seemed gratified by the remark, and the slap she gave Meg's leg was playful.

"Besides." Meg squeezed Alice's waist. "There are undoubted advantages to riding pillion." She raised her hand to a conveniently placed breast.

"Meg!" Alice removed it. "Someone may see us."

"Who?" She scanned their surroundings. The bridle track was deserted. "We haven't seen a soul since we left your father's estate, and it will be an hour or more before my men can tear themselves away from plunder. As for there being anyone in the woods"—she made a show of cupping her ear—"from the birds' calls and the hum of insects, I'll wager no man is within a mile."

The horse checked as a gecko darted out in front of its hooves. Meg pointed at the disappearing lizard. "Or is it his feelings you seek to spare? Or hers?" But the streamer-tailed hummingbird with the red bill was more interested in an orchid growing beside the track than in either horse or riders. "What care they, my sweet, if we kiss and canoodle?" She bent her head to the delicious expanse of Alice's neck.

"Humph!" said Alice, but she conceded the argument by leaning back against Meg, and even moved her hair out of the way to aid Meg's nibbling. "I missed you," she murmured, closing her eyes. "And I missed this." She returned Meg's hand to her breast.

Meg smiled and caressed the swelling curve beneath the silk then slid her hand inside the low cut neckline. "Shall I find us a shady spot?" she whispered, as Alice's colour heightened and her breathing quickened. "Or would you rather wait until we are safe in my cabin?"

"Wait?" Alice swallowed. " 'S blood, Meg, do you mean to torture me?"

Meg laughed and began to look for a suitable trysting place. "My own thoughts exactly. Then a shady spot 'tis."

Barbara Davies was born in Birmingham but now lives in the English Cotswolds. She worked for many years in IT, before becoming a freelance writer and book reviewer.

Barbara started out writing short specfic stories and was first published in 1994. Since then, more than fifty of her stories have appeared in various anthologies, ezines, and magazines. Three of her short story collections are available from Bedazzled Ink.

She now also writes longer fiction in assorted genres. Three of her books were shortlisted for a GCLS (Golden Crown Literary Society) Award, and *Bourn's Edge* won a Goldie for Speculative Fiction. All five of her novels are available from Bedazzled Ink.

Her website is: www.barbaradavies.co.uk

www.ingramcontent.com/pod-product-compliance
Lightning Source LLC
Chambersburg PA
CBHW052144170626
46812CB00004B/1577